Damn Sure Right

DAMN SURE RIGHT

FLASH FICTION BY

MEG POKRASS

Press 53
Winston-Salem

Press 53
PO Box 30314
Winston-Salem, NC 27130

First Edition

Cover design by Kevin Watson

Cover photograph "Knees and Butt,"
Copyright © 2011 by Tom Dolan

Printed on acid-free paper
ISBN 978-1-935708-17-9

For Molly and Doug and Ruth

Acknowledgments

Many of these stories have appeared in the following literary journals and e-zines. I am grateful for their interest and early support of my work:

Juked, Annalemma, Press One, Ampersand, Wigleaf, The Pedestal, Keyhole, JMWW, Rumble, Storyglossia, Mudluscious, elimae, Camroc Press Review, Eclectica, Thieves Jargon, 3AM, Gigantic, Gargoyle, A Moveable Feast, SmokeLong Quarterly, Kitty Snacks, Monkeybicycle, Eclectic Flash, Necessary Fiction, LITnIMAGE, Pindeldyboz, Salome, DOGZPLOT, Metazen, Blink Ink, Matchbook Review, Tuesday Shorts, Prick of the Spindle, Santa Fe Literary Review, Joyland, Night Train, Ramshackle Review, Pank, Everyday Genius, A-Minor Magazine, decomP, and *Women Writer's Magazine.*

I would also like to thank the following individuals to whom I am indebted for inspiration and all kinds of magic:

Ruth Pokrass, Sian Allen, Hannah Davie, Doug Bond, Molly Bond, Barbara Levin, Michael Reuben, Ellery Akers, David James, Cooper Renner, David Woodruff, Grant Bailie, Benita Sachs, Tim Jones-Yelvington.

A special thanks to Dr. David R. Kell, MD for saving my life more than once.

Contents

Damn Sure Right

The man had come up behind me and locked my arms backwards. I could feel his cock or gun against my low back. He told me if I moved he'd hurt me, and he said did I know what that meant? I did know, however I was watching from somewhere else (sort of interested in this, sort of not).

My jaw would not open very well. Two police came and one of them called my boyfriend with his phone. They took a detailed report. When asked, I spit my formal name—blood came out of my mouth but I was not hurt and didn't know whose blood it was.

There was a witness, an African American woman who had been hiding to protect herself. She had helped me up from the dirty concrete floor, straightened my dress, smoothed my hair down. She told the police that she was forty-five years old, employed. She gave them her phone numbers and home address. I felt as if I were watching an actress playing a Good Samaritan in a movie, she was so familiar.

She explained to the police that she had ducked behind a vending cart. She described what she saw him do. She said it was awful, and that he didn't need to do what he did, that I was a petite woman. She told them she had helped me up from the floor, so I could stand on my feet. I nodded my head to show them she had. She said, "He didn't need to hurt her, damn sure right."

One of the policemen asked me if I had family nearby. My boyfriend Ian, I tried to say, but it sounded like "oyfenian." I wouldn't go anywhere without him, I said, which sounded like "ahh wed go widout him."

I wanted to walk up Broadway with Ian, out into the middle of the fine day. I imagined how we would sit at the Greek place, touching. Since I was not compliant with their suggestions for paramedics, they told me that I would have to sign a release denying medical transportation. Did I understand?

How quickly Ian arrived, as if he were there exactly the minute he needed to be—and how still he stood nodding his head while the police were talking. I hadn't yet said goodbye to the woman who had helped me. I wanted to talk to her, but I couldn't see her anymore.

Ian thanked the police and took forms from them. He told me he didn't think we should go to a restaurant. "We need to do the right things now," he said. He held my hand tightly and we walked out of the dim station into the bright afternoon. He hailed a cab even though it was just a few blocks to Roosevelt Hospital.

While Ian filled out admitting forms in the emergency waiting area, I slumped in a chair, watching a plump-lipped weather woman on the waiting room TV. The weather woman looked mildly worried about a tornado, though her forehead didn't wrinkle the way foreheads used to do in the old days. She was moving her arms and hands apart and back together, showing the way a situation with air masses was quickly changing. I hated the way she looked, and couldn't watch.

I said, "Don't leave me" when he got up to go to the men's room. I said it to his empty chair. My slurring words made me feel untidy.

Sometimes now, twenty years later, my husband will enter me from behind—and because I can't see him, I remember Ian—his flannel shirt and the smell of his fear and the things he did that he thought would help.

What They Were Not

I met up with an older boy I had never seen on the road past the bus stop a few times and we got to joking around. Soon it became every day and he would walk me to school. He would point out how certain parts of nature looked like what they were not. I liked the way my brain bent to meet the things he noticed. He did not need a "formal learning institution," was how he explained it. It sounded right, he was smart as hell. He would stand near the edge of the parking lot like one of the crossing guards and watch me walk into the building.

He was an unusual kind of person, a vegetarian with inner smarts, who certain people hated on sight. I had never known a boy with hair like his—puffy and still as a rain cloud. There was a snowbank near my school that looked like a tower of tofu. I remember laughing my head off until he pretended to pee on it. That day I ran ahead.

I imagined him spending nights and mornings at the Shooting Star Hotel, or the Astor, or the Golden Tree lobby areas—reading whatever he could get his hands on, sitting there with his mushroom head. The younger ladies probably liked him, and I wondered what he thought about them. The idea of his toothbrush in a ziplock baggie made me sad and the roots of my hair would crinkle.

4

He said he wanted to leave things in better shape than he found them. The day he disappeared I was looking at the way trees were like shaved carrots. I was better than he had found me perhaps, but I did not forgive him. Every day I saw things more like what they were not. Soon it felt too big—houses were caves in soft sand, dogs were children with hungry smiles.

Her Own Music

After her marriage blew up, Jane's therapist suggested she join an "I Am" class, so she could hang out with other shells of their former selves. She attended her first "I Am" workshop, which was really an unorganized support group with dancing afterward. Jane saw that for most of these people, deep into middle age, music had become a functionality balm, a way to get through the next hour. That and pumping Visine into their eyes. One member started with the Visine, and it began a domino effect, nearly choreographed.

Fiercely addicted to their iPods, the "I Am" members shivered or growled when she attempted to converse. Worse, the men who tried to talk to her after the get-together had mange, or fleas. They scratched at themselves nervously and stuttered.

When Jane dragged herself home alone, thirty new Facebook friend requests glowed in her inbox. She felt desperate for a smoke, had nothing left. If she were a kid she would smoke oregano and pretend it was grass and it would feel wonderful.

Instead, she turned on her own music.

~~~

Jane asked "Tarzan" what he was wearing. He said, "nothing."
She said that she was wearing nothing as well, and that her
name was Jane.

"Good," he said.

"Let's think about something now," she said.

She told him to imagine that they were both in a hot tub,
and it was very comfortable and warm. Jane could hear a
dog barking through the phone, and clearly the man named
Tarzan was chewing an apple or a sandwich. There was the
sound of a toilet flushing.

"So, your cock is just floating like a pontoon boat near
me," she said. "And then, well . . ."

She waited for him to chime in, to say something about
Jane's wet tits gleaming under the full, rising moon . . . or
something.

"So, it's just floating and I'm getting very excited and all,"
Jane said.

She could no longer hear chewing, and the dog had
stopped barking. She didn't hear anyone breathing, and for a
moment, she worried that he may have choked to death.

"You okay?" she asked.

"Yeah, why?" Tarzan said.

"Oh, okay, and so, good," Jane said. She was not naked
but didn't need to tell him that she was really wearing comfy
new pajamas. She needed to cut the tag off the collar, could
feel just a tiny scratching feeling at the back of her neck, like
a flea.

~~~

Jane hired a man from Craig's list named Paul to clean the
pool area, and remove the bees from the water. She liked
Paul's ass, the way his jeans would bunch from all he was
bringing. She really needed to commit to eating red tuna
sashimi for the next three weeks—lunch and dinner. There
were ways to fill days that had nothing to do with fatty food.

There was also a bronze-faced man named Haha; sounded

like a joke but wasn't. The man said he'd had a terrible afternoon, and she had given him the opportunity to accompany her for a seaweed salad. She told him it was "on her," and, sipping Dragonwell tea with him, she asked about the name Haha. He said he had always been a comedian.

Paul was only good at scooping bees, and she couldn't stop wanting to eat seaweed with the dark skinned, funny man.

~~~

At night, after their smoke, nothing would stop Haha's voice, all sucky, burrowing in and out of her fleshy dream and her unstained kimono. In Jane's dream, she was serving tea to young men with shiny hair. In the real world, Haha's voice lived off the blood he sucked from her shins, calves, and her bottom. A tick can draw blood from a person in an ape suit— so hungry, so smart.

Haha's life kept growing, he had hundreds of friends just a click away. He told Jane he was popular because he said things of importance to people. "That's how you collect friends," he said. "Real followers."

When Jane closed her eyes, telephones appeared. They were the only way to connect—she would dial random numbers and say, "Can you hear me? Do you know who I am?" Once, a seven bloomed on her fingers, and she dialed sevens—got a busy signal. Fives felt hungry, maybe fives ate children—so she avoided them. Eights were delightful though untrustworthy, they used Listerine.

Every number had a little problem, and she didn't have anyone but Haha, the size of a dot. Even in her dream, his part of the story needed work—felt false, unfinished. She blamed herself—lived to please. She used his deodorant, his lotions.

He said, over, and over, "Jane is sexy, but she is a real mess." There was one exit, one way to make him happy.

~~~

A year and one day later, Jane met Bill. He was sunning in the yard next door, must have moved in to the rental. She had discovered nettle plants growing, and needed to destroy them before things went further.

Jane had developed a little problem with anything new, in general, since Haha vanished. There is always a loyalty factor, they say, like thread hanging from your skirt, or pocket lint. Where does it come from? Jane tried not to drag Haha's scent behind her everywhere she walked, but somehow she had started tripping. Once or twice a day, she would trip on invisible rocks, or ruts in the sidewalk—undetectable upon later inspection. She would go back like a detective and stare at the place where she'd tripped to figure out how it could have happened again.

Jane's words felt shy. She wanted to say hello across the fence, casually. The neighbor looked sad, sunbathing and reading, as though he were nothing better than an apparition. As if he didn't deserve to be spoken to. Jane understood. This man had large dark glasses and a bald head.

Jane walked over to the fence, cleared her throat, and said, "Hello there." He didn't look over. He might have had an iPod on, in fact she thought she saw white wires hanging down from his ears.

The Big Dipper

The pool was four feet deep, and we bought it at Target half off. You could float on your back and think, "Fun times are here," because at least you weren't burning hot.

Mom and I watched it fill up with hose water. She looked around at the back yard, the neglected fruit trees, and said, "I've got to call those idiots and make sure they get a gardener." It stunk from rotting fruit and dog poop.

I wasn't going to worry about anything. I would just float on my back in my bikini. I would be weightless. There was an annoying flea bite in the crook of my arm, which I sucked on.

The pool was going to be my way of making more friends. I was sick of the two friends I had from last year. Lila and Blythe were both considered to be strange. Lila wasn't ugly when she washed and brushed her long hair—about once a week. She memorized animal facts. Blythe looked like Pinocchio. She was a violin prodigy. She had a European hair cut—short, black, severe. She was proud of her breasts, which were large, adult size. I didn't have any breasts yet, but the doctor said not to worry.

I wanted to know if late development meant small breasts. Mom said it didn't, that she had been the same way. "Worth the wait," she'd say with an exaggerated wink. Now that Dad had his own place and his bi-polar disorder, she had all kinds of new expressions.

In my new pool, I would float on my back when it was dark, looking at the stars. Nighttime swimming had been my dream.

Since there was no one else, I invited Lila and Blythe for a nighttime dip on Saturday. Lila couldn't come because her family needed to drive to Oxnard. Blythe said she sure as heck would be able to make it. She was all about nighttime and pools and stargazing.

"Show me the big dipper," Blythe said. "I want to make sure you know which one it is."

Blythe was wearing her bikini bottoms, but she left her top on the side of the pool. The pool seemed much smaller with her beside me. I was glad it was cheap.

Terribly absent were Lila's cigarettes.

I pointed to the area of the sky where I saw the Big Dipper.

"Uh huh," she said. "A long bent ladle, right?"

Blythe looked wet and slick—her womanly breasts gleaming. I felt angry at her for taking her top off.

"It looks like a crooked dick," I said. The pool was a bee cemetery. I scooped two up and threw them out.

"I don't even really know what a ladle looks like," I added.

I could hear all the neighborhood dogs talking to each other. A bee might have been marching down my arm. Something tickled.

"You know what a crooked dick looks like?" Blythe said. Her face was large, or maybe it was the moon.

"Not exactly," I said, trying not to let my eyes get caught on her nipples, "but I've seen them, and they all have different shapes."

True. I had a subscription to Playgirl. My mother had given it to me for Christmas instead of a new bike. Once she'd found a beat-up copy of The Happy Hooker under my pillow. I'd stolen it from a garage sale. When I came home from school, I found it laid out on my dresser next to my hair brush and retainer case. Nothing seemed to freak her, as long as she had two martinis.

"So, like... whose?" Blythe asked.

"I haven't seen that many dicks, I just have..." If I told her I had a subscription to Playgirl she'd tell Lila, and then God knew what would happen when I stopped being their friend. The water in the pool was getting cooler, the smell of new plastic making things worse. I hoped she hadn't peed in the pool, though I would not put it past her.

"I have a lot of cousins," I said.

She smiled at me so brightly then, she almost looked pretty. She squealed, half laugh, half death cry. She said she was getting cold—hey, what a great idea, let's bake oatmeal cookies.

Suddenly she said, "Could you imagine sucking one of those?"

"God, no," I said, fast and soft. Her eyes looked back at me big, full of thought. She moved in.

"What do you imagine they taste like?" I knew better than to speak.

"Corn on the cob," she whispered into my ear, spitting, "with a bit of salt."

This was not happy news. I knew that violin prodigies lived exotic lives, they were much older than other teenagers. They traveled to Europe.

I imagined Blythe kneeling in front of an audience, her mouth open like a baby bird.

"I'm not ever going to do that," I said. It sounded fake, as if I were acting in a play.

Blythe moved to the far side of the pool. The moving water sounded smooth. She kept still, cupping her chin in her hands. I wondered if our friendship was done.

Her nose was cartoonishly off-kilter, as if a person had sculpted the middle of her face blindfolded. She practiced three hours a day after school, was going to be on CD covers wearing velvet dresses. She was going to be rich. She already knew everything that was going to happen.

The Forever Drive

Turbo asks me if we should go to Burning Man. I say—
"Okay, if you want to drive." So he borrows a van from his
roommate, Mike. It's big enough to sleep in—so boxy we
call it the Rubik's Cube. Me and my breasts the size of goat
heads, sore to the touch. It's the right thing to do, I tell
mom.

She knows. I'd just be sitting at their damn parties being
stared at like a spoiled appetizer by dad's business partner,
Dan Scotty—axe eyed by his third wife, swelling up like Jiffy-
Pop. If I wasn't gone.

On the forever drive to Black Rock Desert from Orange,
we crack each other up, say stuff like, "Say it however you
say it." That type of thing, Turbo laughs so hard he nearly
has to pull off the road.

Dad had a party three months and two weeks ago (one
hundred and four days ago). Dan Scotty bumped into me in
the kitchen, said, "Whoopsy daisy," brushed my nipple with
his forefinger. Then traced a moon around it, real slow.

"You have to stop now," I said to him.

"Your dad's a whore like you," he whispered, sour cream
chip breath and gin, tracing the other moon nipple, like a
piece that fell. That was the first night I let it continue outside

13

by the pool. That's the movie my brain locks down on. When the van growls, it cracks me up again.

I say to Turbo, "Tadpole hill," taking his right hand and placing it on my stomach.

"Moo, moo," he says.

Opening the window to vomit, I feel the rush of desert air. Tonight at Burning Man, I'll cover myself with electroluminescent fake fur so nobody can trip over us.

Pru

"I love you," Pru says during a commercial.

"Me too," I say. It's great not to feel shy with friends, to just say whatever.

We're roommates and buds and amateur therapists. She told me last night I have a guilt complex. I told her she has hopeless OCD. She says, "What do you mean, what do you mean, what do you mean." We laughed so hard I nearly peed.

Jeopardy's on now. We both suck at it.

A car horn sounds. There is a cheer from the college house up the road. Tonight could be loud, so I'll earplug it.

"Wow," she says. I'm looking at the show now, trying to figure out what she thinks is the "wow" thing.

I look at her briefly—she's not looking at the show, she's looking at me. I smile, bend down to butterfly lace my shoe. Out of the corner of my eye I see her face has reddened.

~~~

Carl was a long illness I'm nearly over. Yesterday I stopped crying without the medication. Everywhere I went I used to picture what his reactions would be to people and places, how he'd smile and the air would warm. He'd always known what to say when someone was talking too long—cornering us and rambling. He'd know the polite way to get out of it.

He knew the polite way to break up too—said that he just wasn't ready to take care of somebody.

This morning in Walgreen's, walking near the dye-free antihistamines he uses, I didn't cry but almost fell. The store seemed to be moving, but I didn't see things falling off shelves. Vertigo. I looked it up on the web when I got home.

~~~

At bedtime we turn in. My room faces the courtyard. I get the morning sun, which Pru would just complain about. Pru's room we call "the Cave." My room, "the Mesa." Piles of books.

"Night, Pru," I say from the bathroom after brushing. It's Friday and tomorrow we'll go for brunch like every Saturday. It's what I look forward to. We love the waitress with the Pluto tattoo, who tells us about her hairless cat. Pru will order pancakes and I'll order eggs medium and we always share the delicious hash browns.

In bed I'm on the last mystery in a series. When books end I feel irritable and cut off. I'm slowing my reading and experimenting with rereading earlier chapters between the new ones.

When she knocks I stare at the door for a second. I should have said hey come in idiot face or something casual of that nature in the moment that I didn't say anything.

She opens the door and walks in, wearing her PJs—the ones that make her stomach look flat and long. Her glasses are off and her hair has been brushed glossy.

Pru is prettier than me by a lot. Lanky, angular—a soft profile. She smells like expensive soap—stuff she said I could share whenever. Her mom had sent it for her birthday. She brings the exotic smell of it to the room like she might a snack.

"Shit," Pru says, sitting on the foot of my bed, shaking her head slowly. Her eyes dripping.

"Pru," I say. I don't want anything to ruin brunch

tomorrow. I imagine those eggs, the dark gold potatoes. "Please don't cry."

"I wish I didn't feel this," she says, wiping her eyes on her PJs.

"I'm sick of feelings too," I say, bringing the covers up above and over my body.

She snuggles in toward me, rubbing her hair against my neck coltishly. It feels glossy and ticklish. She gets in the covers. She and I probably look cute—a picture of us could be a Christmas card. Hair down and pajamas and soap smell.

"Have you ever?" she asks.

"No," I say. I should ask her the same question to be courteous—but her answer is so potent now that vertigo sets in.

"I'm on that damn ship," I say.

Pru, my best friend, kisses me—her lips oval and sliding open in a way male lips don't. Opening like a sea anemone. A dark and pretty ocean moment you'd see on Animal Planet, and say to yourself, "Wow." When it's on TV it's safe. What I feel here is not.

I close my mouth and she has to stop. I try not to wipe my wet lips on my sleeve. They are wet when I smile at her, hoping I won't ever hurt her.

The Lobby

My dad in the suite and the TV on, his wine not chilled as he likes, eyelids already droopy and unforgiving. He wants to play Scrabble with me, it's the thing we do at night, but I want the man sitting alone in the lobby who'd looked at me with crackling eyes as though he were an eel. When dad finally falls asleep in his bathrobe and shorts I slide to the red velvet lobby. Eel may be caught between bell boys shifting on their legs, business men loosening their ties; if he's gone, I will find him. I can wait all night in the red lobby full of geeks, listening to elevator bells. I can sit and dream about taking everything away from him.

Pounds Across America

On Tuesday afternoon I line up with other petite brunette actresses, silently, our eyes underlined with dark liner. When it's my turn to walk on stage, the assistant casting director asks me to smile, inspects my teeth for flaws. She has purple hair, a nose ring, and a T-shirt that says 2nd Butch Bitch. She looks me over—back to front to back. Says they'll call if I make the cut.

I work in the fringes of mid-town Manhattan on the night shift, which allows me days to audition. My co-workers are mainly out-of-work actors. Our job is calling people who've ordered our diet product from a TV infomercial.

The floor manager creates a sales contest to motivate us, calls it POUNDS ACROSS AMERICA! We're all nervous, fluttering and bullying each other. I pile Three Musketeers bars next to my coffee. A bite, then a sip, then a call. I wave at Jeremy who's been on the night shift the last month.

The prize is Broadway show tickets for two. I dial, opening my Three Musketeers.

"Yep?" a tired female voice says.

"Hi. Is this Janet?"

"Depends," she says.

"This is Martha Tiffany with Dr. Feldman's weight loss

system! Congratulations, Janet! We've shipped your trial order and you should be receiving it any time!"

"Jingle-jangle-jesus!"says Janet D. Higgins, 190 pounds, in Racine.

"Janet, Dr. Feldman is having us call every customer individually so we can design your unique program. How many pounds do you need to lose?"

I can't help reaching for my Three Musketeers bar. I hear the pop of a fart from the young recruit behind me.

"Fifty," she says, followed by a puff of air.

"Great. How fast would you like to do that, Janet?" I ask, tonguing the caramel nougat.

"Three weeks? Heh!"

"Let's see, I'm just looking at the chart," I say.

I turn to see what's happening. Dawn (who started when I did) is doing her shtick for a group in the back, saying "Pee — niss" in a Mickey Mouse voice. "Pee-niss, pee-niss, pee-niss!"

Janet screams, "Mommy needs a little time out too honey."

"Janet, we're looking at ... (here the script suggests to improvise) ...two to three to four months if you follow the easy step system!"

I look over at Jeremy, his new haircut. He just did a national soda commercial—knows he's hot. He's rolling a joint under his desk, not really caring if he gets caught.

"I got to try something," Janet says. I hear a child yelling.

"Let me get to the other reason I called ... and this has to do with what we just talked about. We care about your success as much as you do, Janet, and we don't want you to have a gap in your continuation—an important concept in weight loss. We're real backed up here, Janet! People are waiting for months to receive orders because of the success they're achieving."

The script says WAIT NOW FOR REACTION.

"Oh," she says. "I guess that's good then. Was your name Martha Tif-ney?"

"Martha Tiffany Reynolds," I say.

I wave at Jeremy near the window grid flipping me off like he always does. I stick out my tongue and he gives me his rat face. We spent last weekend in bed and he's probably bored already.

Janet tells me in hushed tone that I sound like *a super, no B.S. gal.*

"You do too, sweetheart—we love you here," I say.

She says she's a waitress. Her husband died on the way home from work one-and-a-half years ago, crushed by a semi. She has a toddler named Trevor. He's a handful, and needs a good preschool. She hopes to be able to afford one soon.

Sweat is forming under my breasts and pits even though the air conditioning is blasting. I say the last line of the script a bit early, feeling my full bladder, pressing it with my hand to make it worse. "You. Deserve. Success."

She gives me her credit card number, saying, *Shit yes!* to the Supreme Success Package (the most expensive).

"I bet you're pretty and thin, Martha Tifney!" she says before she hangs up

~~~

After work I bring Janet's order sheet home under my shirt. I read off each name as I tear the sheets into bits: Kelly, Nita, Jen, Marla, Iris, Nancy, and Janet. They will be mystified when there's no charge on their statements and they receive nothing else.

I take off my clothes and stand naked in front of the bathroom mirror. Look at myself from different angles. The way a casting director would.

Wrappers

When I started chewing gum a lot, everything changed. I felt better, the jaw movement made me look good. People grew afraid of me, and I got invited to parties. I loved being called on the phone and saying, "Fuck, yeah." Chewing gum until I fell asleep. I had my own room again.

My parents had kicked my cousin April out and she had somehow pocketed my jewelry—had stolen it—which was fine. No, it was better than fine, it was great. She'd look like shit no matter what she put on.

My mom asked me why I hated her. I told mom that she snored, and that she was nosy. My mother had found me at 3 a.m., lying with the dog on the living room rug. She'd heard something that sounded like crying, she said. What was I doing on the floor with Sammy?

I had told her simply that I was not used to sharing a room, and that April smelled bad. "Why does she have to smell bad?" I whispered. My mother said she didn't know—but she was my only cousin, the only family I would have someday when I was grown up, and that poor April had been through "hell" with her mother falling asleep on the highway and dying like that. She said that we could try to be more generous toward her. Sharing was hard for an only child like me, but healthy, mom always said. I was used to it. Mother equated being an "only child" with being born one-legged. She looked guilty as if it were her fault—and I felt sorry for her.

There were reasons to pity April. She was left living alone with her father, my uncle, who worked for a window washing company, had a drinking problem and often got fired. They lived in a trailer park in a dusty town that had no library.

I went back to bed that night trying to be more generous. April was already sound asleep anyway, though earlier that night she had come to my bed right after mother turned our light out. "Looky here," she had said, pulling little bars of chocolate from her PJ pocket—"the most expensive kind, organic, 70% cocoa, imported from Madagascar." She'd already be inside the sheets, unwrapping a bar slowly, watching me watch. She'd break a piece off and extend it with her clammy fingers. "Suck," she'd say, and I did. It tasted special—and she said she'd pin me if I didn't. April was two years older, strong as a man, lean and straight-hipped.

When she rubbed my nipples, she handed me pieces of chocolate and let me use my own fingers. Some nights we went through three bars. Sometimes I forgot what she was doing to me, because it blended in with the taste of chocolate. Those were the good nights. Though, when the hottest days in mid-July started, it got worse quickly, because there was a part of me that itched in a bad way. She knew exactly where, didn't need to bring chocolate anymore. I hated her for knowing what felt perfect.

By the end of the summer she got busted for shoplifting socks, and my mom sent her back to her dad's trash heap. April had embarrassed us in our own community, mother loved to say, had made us look like scum. "Let her live with her dad, that's exactly what she deserves," she said. The thought of her living in a house that wasn't a real house— just a big overgrown camper-car with beds in it, in the middle of nowhere sounded fair.

I craved gum as soon as she left, used all my allowance to buy up every flavor the drugstore had. I would save the wrappers in my jewelry case, line them in alphabetical order before bed like little soldiers.

So I Drew Him a Poodle

I had to stoop to get in because the doorway was caving.
Things didn't look any better inside there, books and papers
were piled obscuring solid objects. I was not in the habit of
visiting freaks, but his cat was gone and that was all he had.
One day I would be sore and old and something I loved
would run away and I would hope for a visitor. I told myself
this, and tried not to breathe with my nose. He drew me a
picture of the cat on a paper shopping bag, said he didn't
have a photo. She looked like a mutant, or as though a dog
had been lodged in her spine. She was half dog and half cat,
kind of like a fox, and I wondered if perhaps he couldn't
draw very well, even though everyone in the neighborhood
said he was a reclusive painter. "Cute," I said.

"No," he said, "she's beautiful." He went to pour some
iced chamomile tea which smelled like dog shit when he took
it out of the mini-fridge. Or, maybe the refrigerator itself
smelled like dog shit, and it wasn't the tea. It could have been
expensive cheese, bleu or raw brie, my mom used to get fancy
brie and the whole house smelled like a thing had died.

He said the chamomile herbs would calm me, that I
seemed all frazzled, and that young people underestimated
this herb entirely. To prove something, he broke a tea bag

open and sprinkled tiny dry pieces of chamomile flowers in a mug. He told me to hold it right under my nose and sniff it as long as I liked.

Sniffing the dusty crap, my head felt plastic, like it might explode. Nobody knew what to say about my mother and her drinking, and I wanted to mention that as the calm came over me. I wished Mom was the chamomile sniffing type, but she wasn't. Also, I knew we should re-focus on the cat.

"I've always wanted a fox," I said, which felt equally important as the cat, and so suddenly.

He sighed, and I realized that he probably wished he'd not ripped a tea bag for me or invited me in. He was going to die soon, I could tell by his gray skin flaps, so I drew him a poodle.

"That was my dog, Stella," I said. He looked at the picture and his eyes watered and he reached into his pocket and pulled out a cracker.

He seemed so naive and plantlike, believing in chamomile herbs, not owning a camera, thinking I had a poodle that died. Mom and I lived in an apartment where no animals were allowed. I faced the door and decided to walk before anything worse happened, before I could tell him or he could tell me that everything was really fucked, had always been and would always be so, even a hundred years from now. Even if we found the cat.

Stone Fruit

It had something to do with shopping and sniffing stone fruit. You, slipping three ripe apricots in your jacket pocket while staring at your ink-black Keds. I wanted to laugh. Instead, I slipped a bottle of coke and beef jerky in my long jacket. Later, you would tell me that we hadn't done this.

Flatfish

Rollicking at night under the waning gibbous moon with Freddy, the dogs bark continuously. One has laryngitis. When they bark continuously, they're just like people.

I have strong opinions.

No I don't. I just mesh with what I'm given. Say you run away with a trickster, a con-artist. Say he's your step-father. Say he asks you to do things you like at first for thrill but you know are wrong. You will only sop up so much, then your long stalks come out. Halt! Don't parcel me out!

Freddy is so gentle he hides behind his hair like an endangered species. Say he sits on a weed, flattens it, apologizes.

It's all about the wispy days of knowing that all you can stand to watch is Animal Planet. That's when you have to leave. Not good. Animals are so much better than we are. Smarter too. When I run away that's what I want to say in my note. Ma has stripped her throat so many times yelling at me that it is dangerous.

Worse than that. Freddy knows.

Flatfish are born with one eye on each side of their heads. One of the eyes begins to move until both are on the same side so they can lie around on the ocean floor and see food. Say this is about how smart nature is.

I'm hiding behind his hair. I'm learning how.

One by One

I wanted a corndog, and had been craving one since my parent's divorce. Weeks. When they split for final and good, I thought about corndogs too often, pictured the skin around the meat, all crisp, gold, and salty. The summer fair was just days away, and I'd get the kind they made there—I could certainly wait for that. I would wear my favorite shirt, the one with three blind mice on it, all of them wearing dark glasses and giving the finger. It accentuated my wide breasts, making them look like frozen yogurt scoops.

I wanted to look as amazing as my big sister did and nothing felt out of place. I wasn't vain, but I had turned out just right, like her. Someday I would get fat and old and married, and would not look this way at all. Would be unrecognizable. For now, I could have what I wanted. Men craned their stiff necks. Women glared.

I hated my house—a blue, shabby stucco. My sister lived in LA, and my dad was gone, but it still smelled like his broccoli. My parents were vegetarians—ate steamed brown rice and millet, had yoga mats, did everything the way they knew they should so as to stay healthy and live long and all that crap. They would tell me how the carnival ride seats would get hot and sticky under my legs if I wore shorts so I shouldn't wear them because that was disgusting. They hated carnivals.

~~~

I cornered my Aunt's husband's boy, Elvis, in the bathroom. He seemed happy about it, but a bit overwhelmed. His egg head turned bright pink. He was two years older than me.

"Tag. You're it," I said. He grabbed a hand towel, and held it over his head while I kissed his lips that tasted like an egg salad sandwich.

"My bike was damp from the rain," he mumbled.

I unzipped his pants and pretended to be experienced. I knew he was not going to hurt me, so I felt him, all the places that I had wanted to feel since my last birthday. Coming back for summers, staying in my aunt's house used to feel familiar and depressing. Now that she was remarried, her old house seemed new again. She'd redecorated and added excellent air conditioning in the bedrooms. I kept an eye out for my cute new cousin, who had a lot of mismatched socks, and wasn't nerdy like the genetic cousins.

"I know we will both need to get amnesia," I said, feeling his body grow like a science experiment. It warmed as well, which I'd never read in any book. It seemed an important detail, that the male organ got all warm and animal-like.

"Sure," he said, putting his hand under my shirt, my bra, feeling my nipple with his calloused finger tip. He was a cellist, which now seemed inconvenient.

"I feel like the dam might burst," he said.

And then it did, and I hadn't even really done anything, it was all about rubbing up against my leg while I warmed it like a hot dog bun. I hadn't really had time to experience the badness of the moment, and now there was a mess, and we couldn't look at each other.

The summer felt ruined. What was wrong with me? I wrote in my journal, but I didn't write anything else about it.

~~~

Things at home changed. I stopped noticing the stains on my clothes, and wore them to school inside out. A brawny boy named Jim felt me up behind the library, and he never cared about any of the things that seemed backwards about me. When he touched the place between my breasts, he'd say, "You need a boy with Armani pants." I didn't know what that meant, but I assumed it was a compliment. He was the only kid I knew who lived in an apartment. There was a device he used to hide his schnapps. It fit inside his jeans, and he said we were part of "The Unsayable" club.

I knew my mother would never drink again if she knew that I was following her down the drain, so I didn't mention it. At night, dinner was a tin can of soup, and we both lost some weight. Mom loved the Bean with Bacon soup; the hickory smell reminded her of camping with her brother, she said. Once she mentioned how he had always been good looking in a crisp way, and when he died, he still was. I had never thought my uncle the least bit handsome, and it felt too easy to glorify the dead.

"Crisp?" I had asked her. "What the fuck does that mean?"

She slapped my face, then she said I would never be an Einstein. There was a wheeze and a puff in her voice that seemed permanent after her last cold. She had never looked so young as she did when my face flew apart.

~~~

The night I almost felt as pretty as my sister, his leg was next to mine and we were in his truck. His banana breath was close. He asked about my sister, did she still love him? I said that I had to think about that, and he said that would be fair, was fair, is fair.

He said we should drive for a bit, and we did, we drove all over downtown. He parked back in the theater parking area, after the silent drive, and I hated thinking about my sister sleeping so much, so hard to wake up.

"She feels like Sleeping Beauty," I said, then felt childish for saying it. He said, he knew what I meant—but he didn't think he was any kind of prince. In fact he was sure that he was just the opposite, that he was a "bad" man.

"Bad?" I said. "Really?"

"Well," he said, "we are all flawed, I guess, but I can tell you this, I have thought about the sad scene of this moment, and many things have occurred to me."

I looked behind me for some reason, then turned back to him. I wasn't sure what he meant, but I could tell he really felt that he was bad.

I sort of scooted toward him.

He said, "Don't ever wish you were like her."

My childhood became a big bag of tangerines, overripe, and I wanted to hurl them at him—one by one. The buildings blurred. I kissed him, and he kissed me back. Then he drove me home, and I never asked God for more.

Crocodilian

"A part of growing old is folding things in half," she said, folding all the kitchen dish towels.

I saw how the family luck, clingy as cat hair, never had a chance to break free. I learned that my mother's luck was a wan cup of Pepsi that has been out all night for a sick child, flat and then discarded. On our stoop, luck cleared its throat like a Mormon missionary and walked away.

Now, the fake flagstone stairs leading up to our house are crazy, and our door knob is black. The sky and the moon always dawdling, absentmindedly humming, doing what the newspapers say.

Her luck was crocodilian, it ate her and I was next in line. I was the child waiting in the shallow water... for soft, tickling fish.

Her luck once had the dreamy lick of salt between us— and then I was born to her... screaming and wanting nothing to do with human milk. I imagine her whisking soy powder into water. The rise of her functional breasts.

We got rid of the dog because he bit the postman. My father left because he hated animals. We still had the three cats. He had a point. I munched carrots instead of crying, my feet and the palms of my hands became orange.

To kill our bad luck, I became the world's best. Best at things nobody bragged about:

1. chopping onions without ruining my makeup.

2. opening a curtain and seeing God in the wet air.

3. brightening my nights by moving things along the softest part of my body.

Luck sways and eats itself. Mom watches less TV and still folds towels. Soon, a boy will find me sitting alone at recess and say, "Hey."

That boy will find me attractive and say, "You are cuter than you think."

He'll try to change my luck while begging for cigarettes, and I'll offer them.

He'll trot to his car to get a lighter, and he'll bring a snack bag of nuts, pistachios... and we'll share them... sitting behind the school library, coughing and munching and kissing, echoing the other's lips.

Puries

He looked like something that belonged to the beach, like moonstones, or fan shells. Riding my bike past his house every weekend in the late spring on my way to the beach—a shiver wrapped its legs around my hips

At the ocean, I sniffed the air for coconut SPF. Sometimes I just imagined the smell, the waves inside my blood. Like when he first told me his name. Peter. I watched him with his long board, by himself. So much tamer than those boys who whooped and tackled each other like village idiots.

At school I was queen of marbles. I'd amassed a coveted collection. I imagined his face while shooting for puries, making everyone sorry they tried. Once, a girl spit at me, called me ugly. She gave me her puries. I held them next to my skin to warm them.

The curvy cool girls (who already wore bras and shaved their hairless legs) sat together eating lunch in a flock. The skinny sports girls played four-square and performed cartwheels and flips, showing off.

I'd started praying near the library:

"Dear God, how are you? I'm fine. Trying to get through this day. Sorry for everything. Love, Eileen."

When my best friend Maria slept over I told her I was in

love for real. "With Peter Doyle?" she asked, in a tone that made me feel I had splattered oil on my own good dress.

"You don't know him," I said, brushing my hair out and tying it into a water fountain shape on top of my head. Wishing I'd never said it.

"He's going with a girl that has big tits. I know from church. Pick someone else." She laughed, slapping her knee at the thought that I liked cute boys, and expected them to like me back. As if it were absurd.

I'd befriended Maria last summer because she was different, dark skinned and real and smart. She didn't play with me at school, because she had tough friends like her. Her parents only spoke Spanish. Maria translated everything they said when I was over, except "hi" and "okay," and "cool." They would say all these words to me with special emphasis. Smiling.

I couldn't fall asleep next to her, wrapped in her sleeping bag like a chrysalis. I reached into the side pocket of her pack, fingered her new turquoise earrings—the ones she got when we went downtown by ourselves. She had a twenty-dollar bill from her grandmother. The man in the jewelry store gave her a quarter back, smiling and polite. He'd wrapped the earrings in three thin layers of cotton, put them in a tiny box with a blue satin ribbon.

I held them in my hand, listening to her doggie snore, thinking about what to do next. Maria wore them every day. I imagined tossing them in with my enormous sack of variety marbles from the dime store. Swinging them around. Letting them ride the waves.

The Happiest Mall in America

I'm at the happiest mall in America, in a food court place called Fields of Cheese.

He is ordering the Goatherd. He says, "Everything...but onions."

I smile at him when he turns around. He's way too skinny, like Scott, like every guy I look at now that I'm fishing in the sea for so many fish. Sometimes I get vertigo.

My shoes are written on. My friends do it drunk and I do it to their shoes too.

He stares at them, and says he likes them. I say, "Better ugly," and that opens things up. He starts yacking but all I can think about is what I heard on the news last night—a report about disease brought on by drought. Like invisible people, these disease atoms seize you and kill you while you are doing something like choosing a pizza and flirting. Maybe you never liked choosing anyway, maybe you wish somebody would do it for you, but you are not ready to die. Some people get into total denial, the news anchor said. Biting their split ends and pulling off the ones that feel broken. He didn't say that, I just know.

Someone skinny like this needs a pillar to lean on, so I smile at him as much as I can without looking desperate. He looks pretty bad with pimpled planets lined up in varied sizes along his chin area.

Scientists say that if humans just splashed sex hormones into each other's faces, we'd heal and live like animals again. Our brains are depressed and taking too many meds just trying to hack into our spirits again.

That was Scott, the police said. His brain was already ruined by the time we met him, and then his body. All the boys I like have little bits of Scott somewhere down inside them, but I have to search.

Skinny kid tells me he's allergic to onions: white, purple, red, and pearl. He doesn't answer my questions.

Still, I'm all ears, over to his table. He blushes like a girl, and soon I'm saying things real soft. So is he—but his things aren't as interesting—the usual. We're whispering lizards, eating stringy cheese together. This is how things start, I say to myself. His eyes follow my mouth, trace my lips. His symptoms are bad, but I won't tell him. He's not even knowing how much is wrong, every little thing that is and isn't.

Weasel

Kurt's family moved in over at the Crawford's house. The Crawfords are dead and buried in the bone orchard, but the house is still there. Her mom says it's rented.

Kissing is Kurt's gift. When his tongue is on hers she decides what his real name is: WEASEL.

She says it to herself, roles it around in the back of her throat.

They are kissing and feeling each other up under a tree down the block from where she lives. His mouth has a different flavor—today it's Coke. She's getting hungry from his taste. Her stomach growls, she hopes he can't tell.

What ever happened to your dog? she asks between wet lips.

Left, Weasel says. She remembers a mangy mutt dog, wasn't the type you wanted to pet. People said the parents had it put down, that it bit someone.

I really want a puppy, she says.

Not one that pees all over the place, Kurt says, touching her nipple. Those are the wrong type.

She feels the sun on her back, water trickles down her arms. Who knows? She may also be the wrong type.

Old woman out walking her poodle under an umbrella

gives them the eye, looks at them sideways. Too long. Sees something and can't look away.

Wait, she tells him.

Woof, woof, he says.

She's sick of worrying about what people think! Pissing fucker, she says very loudly. Her hands thwap her mouth, and she stares at him.

He laughs. Such words from a pretty bitch. Touches her underneath.

Mates

Jim needed a new pair of good hiking boots for a sense of confidence, perhaps. Nothing more. The ones he had were too slim and they hurt. Jenny was gone now, and his time was freed up.

The last thing Jenny had ordered with his credit card on eBay was the essence of acai juice—and it worked. She got mentally well and left him. She had sworn that fresh acai juice powder would help them both avoid the feeling of razor wire after ending the ten-year marriage. Also, Jenny still had Xanax from when her mother died. Jim remembered how she texted him from her mother's hospice every day with little text bubbles that said stuff like, "I miss you," "popping Xanax," and "why?"

On Jenny's and Jim's ninth anniversary, Jim's penis stopped working. It stopped lifting up, and staying strong. It seemed to be broken, and so suddenly.

~~~

After Jenny left, Jim told himself that there were thousands of ways to find a mate in the age of technology—to fit yourself to the person who was in yourself, but with different anatomical parts. He had read it somewhere, said just that way, and it was strangely comforting. Jim got a dog from the

SPCA. Dogs were a great way to connect. He had read that also.

On Facebook, Jenny's profile picture made her look balanced, sexy, funny, and sympathetic. He blamed the impact on the glow effect he knew she used secretly. Even her eyelids seemed luminescent. In life, Jenny was pretty enough.

~~~

When Jim first met Jenny, his eyes felt suddenly and insanely alert. He remembered saying something about how he loved oysters—mainly Blue Points. He felt surprised by her wheat colored hair and the tip of her nose, angular and imperfect. She wore a scent like wasabi. They were at a benefit for the Ecological Sensitivity Society, standing in front of the oyster table, waiting in line. She had nodded, smiling slightly, her head ducked down.

He remembered how much he wanted to show her that, and he did not even know her yet. They exchanged business cards, and he e-mailed her many messages about the different types of oysters and their mystical properties.

"The oceans are half dead, and everything we eat or touch is dead or dying," she said on their first hike date. They were climbing steadily and gradually up Hawk Hill in the Marin Headlands. Jenny sat down suddenly and turned away from him, pulling at the ends of her hair.

She ate tempeh and told him he needed to quit smoking if he wanted to marry her.

He quit, gained thirty pounds. They were married.

They were mates.

~~~

She attributed all human male impotence to the fact that everything was dying.

"The body is honest," she said. He told her he would go to the doctor and get a prescription for Viagra. She was not happy about that—wanted him to try herbal cures for a year or more first. He did. Ginger, ginseng, damiana, saw palmetto, peppermint. He eventually tried royal jelly. It became expensive.

Jenny started smoking and writing erotic poetry about women.

He tried not to think about the easy going, happy Viagra ads—silver haired men with enormous cocks and horny smiles. "Solid metal," one ad said. The model was dressed as a pornographic Tin Man. The woman was dressed as Dorothy. Or did he dream it?

~ ~ ~

The sea of men on the planet... foamy around the edges, something just a little off, stacked in clumps, like muscles.

One night, a year after their divorce, he called Jenny who had been living with a woman named Gerta. He wasn't sure what that meant. Were they lovers?

He said nothing, and could hear her breathing. She said nothing, but she knew it was his number of course. So they were breathing, which felt okay.

Freckles

Loretta, Trina, and Junie were real friends, and their backs were brown as beef jerky. None of them freckled, as I did. Freckles on my face, my arms, my back. Freckles on my lips, flecks of oil, or butter, or tomato sauce on my T-shirts. Everywhere I was spotted, defective. Only the dog's eyes followed me, as if I were banana frosting or a dog's version of it.

Not until my fourteenth birthday did an electric switch turn on. Out came the family neck, the swan neck—as though it rose from my birthday cake where it had been sleeping. My eyes became purple, and boys called them "picture windows." Well, not boys, exactly, but one girl did. Junie. It was still a compliment, since Junie was a ballerina and valued physical beauty, especially the neck above all else—she knew what to look for, called herself a slut. She had an unnaturally gravelly voice, as though she'd been smoking for forty years, as though she were half man, and when she laughed got worse.

"When I'm thirsty I sound like a guy," she'd brag. One night she slept over with her brown back and her dance bag. I became quiet around bedtime, couldn't think of funny stories. She started looking around my room, all nosy, for something to tease me with. When she crawled under my bed I could see her bellybutton popping, an "outie," like a Cheerio.

"Is this your little teddy bear?" she asked, she'd found Ted, my childhood pal, a ripped stuffed bear with a babyish face behind the plastic storage boxes. Holding Ted by the neck, Junie was trying to make him squeak like a dog toy. I wanted to ask her advice about how to change my personality, how to become tan without wrinkling up and dying from skin cancer. Anything felt possible.

I slid next to her so she wouldn't rip Teddy up, kissed her for a long time to save him.

The Ladybug Orgy Tree

I am not taking painkillers, though they say I should be. Everything hurts but not enough to do anything to stop it. When the tree branch fell, I could not see the ladybugs mating. Dan's head was squashed, and not the way a cartoon makes it seem.

Once a year, we went to see their orgy. One tree had more ladybugs than any other, and drew the largest crowd. People called it the Ladybug Orgy Tree.

"Do you remember who you were with?" one of the doctors asked. I was hurt but not killed. I wasn't ready to say Dan's name out loud. It felt like a careless bubble, his name, from my lips.

The world is tilting and this is well known. My aunt who has more money than God insists I go away to a healing camp. On the phone she says, "Do what you need, you shouldn't even be here, you are a dot of light."

She is a manic depressive and interesting and loves me. I attribute most people's kindness toward me to some kind of mental disorder.

There is a rustic village in the mountains where people vacation to "get over" things, and that is where she wants me to go. People make pottery and nap and bring their own personal sound soothers.

She sends me a video of the place—it features a big solid looking wooden lodge-like room where people gather to "boost social endorphins." The title of the video is "Connecting Mindfully." Men and women move and smile, touch each other's arms and play cards with sealed smiles. I stare at a dark haired man with glasses, clutching playing cards in his hand, spreading them out like a fan. "Haw, ha, ha," a woman's voice crows.

In pictures now, I love Dan's glasses more than I did when he was alive, and further, I love that he looked completely different underneath them. I can't kiss him because he's far away and possibly worse, and it feels like the earth breathes smoke sometimes.

Outer Lands

John said so, even before we built our home by the ocean—
there would be nothing but wind and sand. It gusted so hard,
and often.

John had warm palms, covered my icy fingers for hours
some evenings. I sketched his big rough hands: Sometimes
they were pinecones, other times baby rabbits.

My hat blew off my head, two thousand times, tiny grains
of sand filling the spaces between hair follicles, catching in
the corners of my eyes. Nothing wanted to grow in such
sandy soil, nothing took root.

John, he watched the ocean with his face a Bible, brought
me a kitten he found in the dunes. Took to working seven
days, hired a hand, this routine attached to that routine.

The wind tricked us too long.

Spit dropped from the clouds onto my face—sand so
fine invaded the seams of my boots.

In my mind he called me "evening."

He started to carry pots for me, then dishes, then the cat.
I couldn't bend to pick her up the day she died, so he said
he'd take her. I watched from the window while he lifted her
curled, carried her to the water.

Team

Because people are used to getting what they want from her, the dogs have become a team, she is their leader and even that is a lie. When nobody's around, she trots after them. She used to have a job answering phones, but got to hating people by their voices, disconnecting them. She thinks about small things now; biscuits, leashes, bags. The nervous Lab in her walk group. There is always a story inside a story inside a dog. She wakes up believing that all she wants, really, is a man's wet, brown eyes.

Her Bottom

Haley was lovely and talented and it was hard to be her best friend. We were both students in our first year at a small acting conservatory. Her hair shone—had an impossible silkiness. She'd whip it around and make a soft tent for herself when she was feeling low. I used to pet it like an animal.

Every physical feature was doll-perfect—except for her large, round bottom, which gave her character. It seemed to smile, as though proud of being her only flaw. She covered it with long sweaters.

Her boyfriend, Ray, went bowling weekend nights with his friends—and she took it personally. She had her hair highlighted, bought books with titles like, *Foreplay Facts*. He didn't believe in self-help books. She'd tell me how much sex hurt with Ray—like it did the night he took her virginity away. She said he was tired of her complaining, was tired of *her*, and she didn't know what to do about it. Wasn't sex supposed to be pleasant? Was there something physically wrong with her?

I remember saying, "Don't worry. When Ray calms down and can really love you, it will feel different. It will."

"He might be gay," she said. "Gay or bi. Nearly all the men here are."

From personal experience, it was hard to agree—but I did. Persimmons were in season, so we bought one, cut it open, and tasted the Fall.

She won every good role, and all the students were jealous. I defended her, saying Haley was the only one of us who could pull it off. Wendy in *Peter Pan*, Liesel in *The Sound of Music*. Her father knew the artistic director, Byron. She let everyone know where she and Byron dined, how he would nibble cocktail shrimp from her salad. Byron never addressed me, probably didn't even know my name.

She showed me a picture of her father in his movie producer suit, dark glasses, cardboard forehead. Her step-mother, his second wife, a dancer, all golden and tan. Long. It's all plastic, she said, one afternoon, pacing. She said she hated the Jewish act her step-mother put on during the holidays, the phony way she'd say, "Oy, so svelte!" She begged me to come home with her.

~~~

Twenty years later, I watch Haley's show in its fourth season on the Disney Channel. The way she says "gawd" gives her away, though she is a stick now. Without her round bottom, she has no character. I imagine it rising and deflating, snug in a box in her attic, along with our letters. Her forehead is cardboard. She plays the part of the teenage star's sarcastic, hip mom.

She smiles at her daughter, says, "Honey, sex is wonderful, but only when it's time." Her daughter, played by a famous teen actress with blown-up lips, nods. "Or not," Haley says. The canned laughter cuts like a cake knife. My dog beats his tail near the front door, needing to pee.

Haley kisses the teenage actress on her lustrous head. "When you love someone, everything changes. I promise, it will." She is using my inflection, my voice.

She Wanted a Dog

Her daughter was shy and reclusive. Her husband had wanted a son. Her family seemed downtrodden and anxious. They were a small family of three—fastidious. She thought about the idea of bringing home something furry with hot breath that didn't come with an elaborate set of instructions and warranty options. She pictured her husband and her daughter at the beach with it, throwing it a Frisbee. The agile dog catching it in his mouth and running, running, running. Her family battling their brittle nature, chasing each other on the sand. The three of them laughing over the brown paw prints on the beige rug after a walk with the dog. They could care less, they would love that dog so much. She could see it in her mind and even smell the dog on her hands.

She also knew she was lying to herself. She remembered how it had been hard on their relationship when she had rescued a parakeet during their courtship. He hated knowing the miserable bird was captive in their one room apartment, watching. Fucking became strange and self-conscious. As predicted, the bird became quiet and lost most of its feathers.

Finally, she gave it to a cab driver out of desperation. They didn't break up, but they never spoke of it again.

Scraps

Ma says *stand back* while she strikes the match, lighting the Wedgewood stove. There is an end-of-the-world whoosh as gas and flame mate—*omelets out of scraps are keen,* she says, sucking a Menthol—arranging button mushrooms as eyes, red onion slices into tight little smiles. At dinner, my sister's hair hangs like a thick curtain around her face. Sometimes I'll poke through it, whispering, *how much for your last three bites? A dollar,* she'll say. Ma can even make a piece of cooked cow look lovely, we both agree, trying to raise two children on her own. My sister excuses herself for the bathroom after dinner. Mom and I look at each other as the sink hisses, then the angry toilet joins the music. We pass the time by inventing situations, playing two truths and a lie.

Cobb

First he just wanted Italian dressing. Then he said, with bits of egg, chicken, and avocado.

"So you want a Cobb?" I said, noticing his alien looking sneakers—the kind with coils in the heel.

"Let's not name it, OK? Let's just say, 'customer X' wants an eclectic salad of greens, egg, avocado, chicken, with an oil and vinegar dressing. Dig?"

He seemed so reasonable, with his cocked head, silver framed reading glasses sliding down his nose—a look of awareness.

"I'll do my best," I said.

"Oh," he said, "and I hope you have greek olives."

I smiled, put my hands on my hips.

"Really," he said, "it would mean a lot."

I went to check out what I could do, feeling his eyes on me for a few seconds as I turned. When I got to the kitchen, I asked Chet, and he said, "Fuck this prick. What's next. Capers?"

I said, "Fuck yeah. Jerk."

Chet said, "Tell him it's $2.00 extra." I kissed him on the cheek and smelled red wine, though not as much as yesterday at this time.

I went back and he was on his phone.

I wasn't going to stand there waiting, so I slipped off to table five. Two eye-locked women. One big one with a lip ring, five brow rings, and a "Save the Bait Dogs" T-shirt. A little skinny blondie twirling her coily hair with her index finger, smiling and giggling.

"Everything OK?" I said.

"Rock on, Dracula," the scrawny one said in a king crab voice, her lips quivering like a hummingbird.

"Good," I said, trying not to flip them off, needing a quick bathroom break.

In the mirror, my eyelids sagged from pollens and lactose exposure. I did the "big eyes, little eyes" exercise. Neck rolls. I moved my rib cage in circles like a boa. Still, my face and upper arms looked just like my mother's, and my grandmother's. Meaty and loose. No matter how many minutes I jogged, attached the pedometer on the late night and morning shifts.

I checked anyway, just for fun. Fifteen thousand steps. If I let myself think about it, there might be a stabbing feeling between my third and fourth toes.

Alice-In-Wonderland Syndrome

When I wake up, I'm not as small, but my jaw is stiff, and my neck hurts. I've been hurled through space again. I can focus on the dresser stacked with books, my apricot velour skirt waiting to be ironed, folded on the chair. I hear a car honking, someone yelling, "Ray-chell." Which isn't my name, because Rachel is a little girl with a hoola-hoop who lives next door. She has a blow-up beach ball that looks like planet earth, and loves to show me the different continents, tell me how global warming will effect the humans who live on them— who will die first in what type of natural disaster.

When I look in the mirror, I see a sour-faced woman, no longer a girl. There is a clicking sound when I yawn, my jaw telling me it's time to squeeze through the rest of the day.

Today I'm a rabbit, yesterday I was an industrial crane. "Good grip," my mother told me, when I said what I'd discovered about my symptoms on the Internet. She doesn't believe in crazy-ass syndromes, so I don't tell her anymore how small I become in the middle of a regular day, and how large my fingers look—heavy as a truck. How, sometimes, the dog is bigger than me—and I am not frightened.

Hinky and Claudette

Max returned the rats in their little traveling cage, and I nodded. We were more often apart now, but he'd borrow them for visits. Hinky and Claudette, silly rat names.

"Listen," Max would say. "I have to meet Paula and deal with Costco crap!"

He gave me a brotherly kiss and two new rat hammocks and his eyes lingered briefly on mine. People were more fickle than rats. My mother left my father, and before my father she left my sister's father.

List: How to Get Through the Holidays:

1. Sedate self and go to parties.

2. Avoid men and make them sad.

3. Spend afternoons in museums looking for paintings with small animals.

4. Give the rats soy milk from a dropper for their holiday treat.

"Nobody can inject you against this crap near the holidays," Max said. I agreed and tried to laugh.

Paula was born as a handy shopper, he explained—she had a mouth full of the right words and healthy reflexes. I imagined Max pushing her speedy-fast in his supersized shopping cart through the aisles of Costco... her hair flying and her mouth saying "Wheeee!"

Drunk Elephant

Elephant, I said, looking at his flash card with an ink splotch. *It has a trunk or a curly leg.*

Oh, the doctor said. *Okay. Yes. And what is the elephant saying or doing?* he asked.

It's drunk, I said. *This may be the kind of elephant that looks for ways to get high! I* said. *This is real, this really happens—I read about it in a science magazine,* I added.

You must know this elephant! he laughed.

I thought the doctor looked really striking in navy blue. His eyes were the color of a humid jungle sky.

So, what about this here? he asked, holding up another ink blotch card.

Sharpie, I said. *Hm. Well, that is a sharpie or a penis. It could be either thing, but it looks very friendly—as though it could make someone really productive or smarter than they are,* I added.

I looked at the clock in his office. It was broken or time was moving too quickly. I loved being asked such weird questions, slyly teasing him about Freud and penis envy theory, and I liked the doc's ageless smile and his tilted green eyes.

San Francisco, he said. *Thank God we live in San Francisco.*

He laughed. I laughed. I had no idea what he meant.

Why do you say so? I asked.

Well, he said, *I'm not sure exactly. It just came into my head. I mean, you have very unusual thoughts. It's a compliment,* he said.

He looked at me as though he wanted to ask me a question. His eyes were purple today.

For someone with an inoperative tumor, I had a pretty good sense of humor. He had a good sense of humor too. I was proud of us for having good senses of humor.

A shaft of sunlight trickled in through the skinny, tall window and lit up the doctor's face. For the first time, I noticed an asymmetrical mole on the right side of his cylindrical chin.

Misshapen—blue and black and gray.

He fingered his mole with his index finger. I squinted at it hard.

I want to talk about the shape of that, I said.

Go ahead, then, he said. His right eye took on a tiny twitch.

He opened his desk drawer and pulled out a hand-rolled cigarette. He lit it, sucked strongly, and handed it to me. It felt strangely normal taking it from his hand, sucking on it, holding the smoke inside my chest. The room became quiet and cozy.

I told him that the shape of his mole looked like the shape of a continent.

Which one? he said.

This had something to do with drunk elephants and what I had read about pleasure-seeking mammals. Smoking, passing it back and forth. After ten minutes or so, his mole became a smudge of dark chocolate.

Jezus in the Backseat

Tara Googled a movie of a naked man standing on a fire pit and not screaming. Smiling. She didn't know how he did it. She Googled "man standing on fire and not dying," and she Googled "schtick." Nothing came up. Tara went to bed after that and could not sleep—and the next day, she agreed to the contest, which was running barefoot to the recycling cans in Ginny's yard. It was a trap, and old Ginny won.

Tara thought she would never agree again to a contest, would be just fine if she had a different, less-girly voice, a lower voice—and the rest of her would make sense then. The full breasts and wild hair that people said was kinky. If she could stop squeaking when she tried to argue, also.

Maybe it was about having porcelain skin and looking fat in five mirrors out of five. Why did she think her stepdad was watching her put on blue sparkle shadow in the hall mirror when it would take a flood to rise him from the recliner? His one shoe off, his bad foot swollen and raised, the TV remote on his lap. Did he think she would even try to grab it? Tara's mother on the night shift and her makeup case loaded like fishing tackle.

Ginny was acting impressed, because they got picked up in a car that belonged to Jezus's parents. Tara could see the

Jezus shit right away, the minute she saw his long hair. The dude said "Let there be light" when he saw Tara. He was her booby prize. His smile looked like hell on earth. The car smelled like honey and cat food.

Ginny got the one with the Brazilian accent. Christ Almighty asked Tara if she'd ever worn a water bra. Tara said to herself, "Kiddo, kiddo" as she took what he gave her from his hands. She hoped they were clean. Next, his paper lips over her shoulders because he was "impressed" with all he could see.

She let the son of God unhook her land bra. Her wireless bra, she joked, but this guy did not know how to laugh. Mostly they did know how to laugh, but this one was too looney. And his hair seemed to come off in her fingers.

He had such low eyes and green shadows on his cheeks. The Brazilian and Ginny were giggling outside of the car and Tara was lying in the back seat. She would do this for all the people in the world who never ever won contests. She was fine already, a naked waif in God's eyes. Tara said this to herself—and like her mother coming home to a sleeping drunk man in the TV chair early in the morning, she would not grit her teeth.

Like a Family

The city is always moving its pinkie to tell me it's alive. One day it smells like steaming artichokes—another day, lapsang souchong tea. My friends, other secretaries, gather on the sunny bench like a bouquet. From a block away it looks as if they are complaining, bending backwards and yawning. He never liked them, or even wanted to know them, but now that he's not around, they're what I have.

I live on Carl Street near the park in a room big enough for myself and maybe a ferret, a half block from the express train. I work downtown in an office complex where I keep schedules for three generations of architects. For Christmas they gave me a robot dog, and a gift certificate to TravelSmith.

My stomach twists like an earthworm after the rain. I tell myself I won't wait for the phone to ring anymore, but have waited all Saturday morning again. When it rings, I count to three, touch "talk."

"Yo Yo Ma," I say.

Calling me is probably on his "to do" list, which I imagine includes trying on new running shoes in preparation for his next marathon, meeting his training coach in her live/work space, upgrading his phone or his GPS running gizmo, catching up with his ex-wife over Dragonwell tea. Taking the kids for the weekend, so she can play.

"What's new?" he asks.

He's lighting up—I can tell because his breathing sounds ragged and doggy. Rain starts drumming on my roof. I look at the ceiling, which seems to be sagging in on itself. It's not my ceiling, so let it crumble.

"I miss you at lunch," I say.

"The world is your oyster," he says. He said the same words when I told him my period was late, very late, and that we had a pink color from it all. Still, he said, he was moving to London to help raise his elementary school kids. The main thing, he told me, was that his brother would never fire me— that I was like family. As long as I remained with the firm. His cheeks looked puffy, like he'd just received Novocain.

"So we're a firmly?" I'd said, blood warming up my face like a space heater that really worked.

He didn't laugh. He never laughs.

On the phone there are silences and delays—words that could have been taken from flash cards. My voice echoes back at me, and I hate the sound of it. I imagine the glow of his cigarette littering London. I hang up and it all comes out. After I clean my mouth and face, I take a walk.

Freaky Forty

Toni's girlfriends were jealous, so she assured them Tommy also had male problems, like their guys did. Peeing more than he used to, stuff like that.

Nobody fucked with Tommy. Nobody could argue with him, he was always reading books and learning facts. Also, he took male baking classes and naked yoga on weekends. There were classes for men to learn to cook and bake at the Town Center mall, and next door there was the Yoga Melt Studio. Tom was proud of being a man who could bake and stand on his head naked, and not many people could argue that he had unique gifts.

"Freaky forty," he said about his botox treatments.

They didn't talk about the thirties, which had to do with fertility clinics and skinny, young medical clinicians, new ones with blue eyeliner and bright hair.

"Who is the Godfather of Soul?" was the type of question Tom asked while she started the dishes, before Jeopardy.

Toni knew the answer, but couldn't remember the guy's name. She could never remember names, was up all night looking at different ways to fuck, rated by spiritual enlightenment charts. There were some ways to fuck that can make both people levitate. There was a photograph of this phenomenon, though to Tony it appeared fake—the woman's head so much smaller than the man's.

California Fruit

We were transplanted Pennsylvanians who understood the value of fresh fruit. The rental house had lemons, oranges, tangelos, loquats, figs. My mother let me take the bedroom that faced the orchard.

I saw him the second week. It was the middle of summer. He lay on a striped beach towel between our two yards, near the loquat tree. I went outside to say hello. I was not exactly shy, though my voice sounded it. An elaborate coconut scent surrounded him. He smiled and asked me to join him. He was tanning, though his body was already brown.

I went inside for my SPF-50 Coppertone, grabbed a beach towel, and went out to where he lay. I asked what his ancestry was, admiring his black tilted eyes and dark, thick skin.

Sioux, he said. He was one quarter Native-American, one-quarter Spanish, one-quarter French, and one-quarter Norwegian. No surprise that he'd been exotically grafted.

He told me not to put on the sunscreen, offered me his wonderful smelling basking oil instead. He said I was pretty, but would fit in better with a really good tan.

I burn quickly from the sun, and mother had warned me not to try. My dad never told me to be careful about anything, but he was dead now. I knew that Mom's voice had gotten too strong.

He told me not to worry about sunburns, assured me that my freckled skin would adapt, just like his. He asked me if I would be interested in meeting him again that night when our parents were asleep.

Climb out a window and you'll make no sound, he whispered, as if there were spies in the loquat tree.

That night I put on my nightgown and went to bed. My skin was stinging and bright red. When I touched it, it turned white for a second, then bright red again. I took two aspirin. I couldn't wait to see him again, under a softer light. I was not too young to understand what this meant.

Under the night sky, he looked as dark as a hazelnut. His eyes were thirsty. We started laughing about nothing, rolling on the ground and grabbing the grass—flicking it at each other.

It's warm tonight, he said, unbuttoning my shirt.

He ran his hands over my breasts, my stomach.

What's here? he whispered. He put his finger inside my bellybutton, and scooped out a small fruit seed. He laughed.

I went crazy eating tangerines today, I said. I was glad it was dark because my face felt hot. It seemed I could not get enough citrus flesh.

Juice, he said, moving his fingers inside my jeans and into a place I couldn't believe.

~~~

The next night we met again. When we took off our clothes, he stroked my irritated skin curiously, as if offering first aid.

Soon you'll get tan, then brown, then perfect, he said.

What is it with the tan thing? I asked. I really wanted to know.

He flinched and stiffened. My skin got cold.

Bugs, he said, swiping at the air. I realized my family's bad fortune could slip over me like a dark curtain.

We lay silent for a while listening to the sounds of night.

I decided to tell him about a friend of mine... a girl I knew, whose father insisted their family move to Alaska. He worked for the telephone company because that was where the money was.

She's never even had a boyfriend, I said.

Or fresh fruit, he added, bringing my hands to the place above his thighs. We did things new to me that I'd never forget.

~~~

A week later, he disappeared. I found out that he'd been visiting his aunt next door. He lived somewhere in Wisconsin. I had been so sure he was a Californian... that meeting his strange expectations meant belonging.

It was our first winter in California—just Mom and me. No cousins, no aunt and uncle, no grandparents to visit. I sent them postcards of my beautiful new land. Pictures of palm trees lined up like chorus girls. Huge waves and white beaches. Bikinied women the color of the dark pine furniture we left back home.

My chronic sunburn peeled in tiny pieces like snow.

Brain Chemistry

I was drumming the "William Tell Overture" on my throat with my bony fingers, and that skill made me feel superior. We were having a sleep over, and playing roles that felt real. "The nurse" (my best friend, Julie) was thin-waisted and she had tiny broomlike arms. I remember flipping around on the bed and playing the nutty patient in the psychiatric ward. The nurse looked like she was always witnessing a disaster, and was threatening to quit nursing. She would say, "They do not pay nurses enough money!" This role made her feel superior. Since we both felt superior, neither of us had a problem feeling worthless.

Unlike Julie, I actually liked a few boys. I mentioned this when Julie had me pinned down on the bed and was tickling my shoulders with the ends of her long unruly hair. I liked the boys who were direct about what they wanted from me, and the ones who admitted that they wanted to have my mouth very close to them, and I liked the boys who were pleasant with their lips.

"Gentle Jesus," I said, even though I had a growing suspicion that Jesus was far from gentle, in fact the Jesus I knew was very fierce, quietly sexy. Recently I had begun to touch myself and think of his eyes and his chiseled nose. I would ball up some socks and move them around between my legs and feel sort of holy and grateful.

Just thinking about this made me want to change my brain chemistry. I reminded Julie of the cabinet in the garage where we could get what we needed to make the night really fun, the place where my father stashed his Jim Beam. Dad did not believe in religious stuff, he called Jesus both a faker and a fraud, like president Reagan. Dad was often in court for driving bad. He called his bottle of liquor "my holy slap of delight" as though holding it was like bringing first breath to a newborn.

Julie didn't say anything about the Jim Beam. Her silence felt like the outcome of something bigger. A poem by Shel Silverstein about obedience came to mind, and I remembered how much Julie and I had loved it. Shel was our man, our poet daddy, our friend. He was what we were about. Her quick laughter no longer seemed unguarded but instead resembled something like snotty gurgles.

"Jules…" I said, "what is his real name anyway? Sheldon Silverstein? Why was he called Shel?"

Julie sighed. She moved to the far side of the bed and sucked on her fingernails while she thought.

"'Cause it makes him sound small and perfect?"

Jules looked pointier and more serious than she had just yesterday, her face delicate and slightly off-kilter. It was my turn to be the nurse.

Moon Honey

We eat beans and rice, and try to take into account the radar bouncing around Reno, the biggest little city in the world, or the littlest big city in the world. We have a room at The Homestead Motor Lodge—free movies and Wi-Fi.

"We're pioneers," he says. He smiles and I try to copy him. "Some honeymoon," he says.

My words are hiding and my throat feels sore. I sit Indian legs on the floor, trying to beat the dizziness. Focusing on a roach near the door.

I remember how, when we first started, he poked at my breasts with his fingertips and said, "These are real."

How he inspected the network of moles around my neck. They are an oddity—and have been good for conversation most of my life.

"How many eggs for women in life?" he asks.

There are tarantulas next door. The room is shaking.

The dial-up preacher said it this way: "Love is similar to the voice of God, and a very, very, very special fruit." Each "very" he said softer than the one before it. I imagined bruised mangos.

Perhaps he has more poetic vows to say for those who upgraded from "White Rose Basic Vows."

"Are you on space, moon honey?" he says, flicking on the tube. It is an adult channel and three women are tonguing each other's ears.

Extinction

"Honey bees are dying because of atmospheric electromagnetic radiation," she says.

She says this while she rubs his back. Then she kisses the hair below his neck, where it comes to a point between his shoulder blades like a heart.

"What happens in the world, and across the street exactly?" he says, fidgeting.

She can feel him stiffening, and she is going to wait, but not forever, not too long. An asteroid could hit, is likely to hit... any minute. The Big One, the nine-pointer on the San Andreas fault is looming like an angry landlord.

"Feed me immediately," he whispers. "Feed me for I am God. I am the Internet."

"I will call you Wiki," she says.

"Did you see the update? There is a gunman with lips pointing toward a man's waist." She kisses his waist, and he knots his fingers deep into her hair.

Species dying every two seconds. Breast cancer multiplying and dividing and running triathlons—making women hate their own lovely breasts and praying for male children so they won't have breasts to poke and worry about and the ozone ripping apart and melanomas on white cats' faces.

She rests her head on his thighs. He lips her nipples, licks them. She moans a bit.

She is a dangerous person, a person who has been treading on the flagstones of men with wives and kids... but this does not stop her from wanting.

Surrogate

He sent her a touch-and-talk parrot, named Goldswack. They still hadn't met in person, though he said he loved her soul, and she said she loved his.

The face of the parrot looked like the face of sex, all beaky and ecstatic and involved with its own satisfaction. She placed it high on top her dresser, above everything else.

With the captain in mind, she lay down topless and bottomless, thinking about tobacco, pipes, and parrots. Blocking out elliptical machines, hormone patches, and Skinny Cow popsicles. The pattering of new rain put her to sleep for a mid-day nap—and while nothing wonderful slid up or down any particular crevice of her body—when she awoke she felt as though she had been somewhere exotic.

Tenders

He said to meet him in the Tenders & Muffins at lunchtime, that he couldn't say why, which made as much sense as the fact that cat urine glows in the dark, which it does. I pulled out my phone to see if he had texted, but he hadn't. My phone looked like the cockpit of a plane, and I understood how to make it do hundreds of wonderful things. It was the only object I loved and trusted.

At lunch, the waitress came over and looked at me hard, as if I'd just been playing with somebody's dick—women looked at me with anger more than I could understand. I always smiled at them, but people are animals and none of us get why we hate each other.

He sat down and said he was very hungry.

"Thank you, thank you, thank you, thank you for coming here," he said. "Did you see anyone else from production? Is anyone from production here?"

I loved his belly, and wanted to take off my shoes so I could warm my toes on it.

"Nope," I said. "Nope, nope."

"I'm going to tell you too much now," he said, then signaled the mean-eyed waitress and ordered two Polar Bear sandwiches and one garlic fry plate. "We can share," he said.

"I would like that," I said, wishing I had brought my Emetrol, which makes me feel all cozy and taken care of instead of nauseous and bad.

The urge to pee was knocking or was it nausea, sometimes it all felt the same. I could see he wanted, no, he needed, all my attention.

It was time to say something that would fix him. Why did smells bother me so much?

"How tiny..." he said, looking at my folded hands, his face pinking from hunger, or from lust, or from depression. He knew that I went to three meetings a day in three different neighborhoods so I wouldn't have much time for small talk, and this was something we shared. There seemed to be a magnet between us, stuck and pretty.

I looked at my hands, and they had veins like my grandmother's hands.

The waitress asked us if we would be ordering dessert. I said we would split a hot fudge Sunday with whipped cream and nuts. She smirked and nodded. In the bar I could tell what the movie was, it was the one where people became flies and killed each other.

Underneath

Her mother said they were starting up again, like in books and movies. The first thing she noticed in California was this: the underside of things often look cramped, like a shellfish inside the opening of shell. She would never touch snow again. She could watch it in the distance, glinting and winking from the mountains every other year or so. She had Jasmine, Eucalyptus trees, small butterflies. Smells that overwhelmed her with the feeling of "lucky," though she didn't believe it. If she walked in snow, just once, she might be whole again, the feeling of snow and going from cold to warm inside.

The thrill of pony rides, the quiet of a tourist park in October. The feeling that her father is looking for her, but she can't remember his face. Growing up on the warm beaches, her belly button as open to the world as an eye, watching for trouble. Boys were called, "Conch" and "Bong." They rode the waves, and she watched.

She would scream on the weekends, throw shoes at her wall. Her mother's problems itched like dry skin. She sank a wooden leaf, imagining it was her father, and still it floated. Later, trouble had something to do with the light in her walk-in closet, the smoke from patchouli incense holding her still.

Music tinted the air with who she was, who she had become. Soon, she would be meeting another boy, not her boyfriend, by the creek at midnight. The honeysuckle flowers would have already bloomed, and she would teach the new boy to suck out drops of honey from the stems, on the lawn. She would show him how to be that gentle, to get the drop to come out just right.

Everything Surprises Me

I remind her that we were a couple who had once lived up six flights of stairs.

I remind her that we were in the farthest apartment.

I remind her that perhaps I had always had a bad memory and always will and that, still, everything surprises me.

I remind her that I feel too much like my mother after I eat a lot.

I remind her that certain sounds people make when they eat sickened her.

I remind her that television didn't interest us at all, in fact, we never turned it on.

I remind her that her knees were lousy.

I remind her that we are all alone with these things.

I remind her that a human can take you with them, and there is no way back.

I remind her that there are worse things than being adorable.

I remind her that she was crossing the street before the light was actually green.

I remind her that her scent is still in the closet.

I remind her that I go for walks.

I remind her that one day I'll smile in my sleep.

I remind her that she should wait for cars to pass.

The Magician

I wake at dawn when he chants, bangs his mini-gong. His mouth is wide, lips so flexible they could swallow a rabbit. I'm afraid to jinx anything, climbing out of his low futon, don't try for conversation.

"Talk is breaking many rules, but listening is holy," he said last night when he sawed me in half but didn't.

I listen to him listening.

The city smells salty, orange light sneaks around his shower-curtained window, cabs call like geese, or mothers of missing children.

"Break a leg tonight," he says, kisses my mouth.

Them

You would hate it if you knew how many times I apply lipstick now that you're gone. I'm putting it on, like, every five minutes to get through the next fifteen, though I know they use fish scales to make it, and it's like killing fish to put on lipstick for no reason. Nobody usually sees my champagne-grape stained lips except myself, and two adorable medical professionals.

If I had been a cat you probably would have kept me forever, even with an incurable disease. I think about that every time I clean the litter pan, especially late at night. I clean it too often because it makes the cats love each other more, and also because I can smell how sad I really am in the unpleasant odor of their piss, which I've read glows under black light.

In bed, my eyelids behave like cheap polyester drapes, unable to keep out the light. I wake from dreams about us walking nowhere... covered with butterflies. I can taste you with my feet the way butterflies taste leaves and flowers. Without you here, I notice too much about how the town is changing, new money moving in, teenage girls with their rubbery, flat stomachs. They walk around cold-eyed, like billboards about nothing.

Sometimes, I drive to the Taste It where they use organic

bags. As I shop, I try not to gawk at girls' stomachs like I used to try not to stare at perfect front lawns. If I had a flat stomach, and a perfect lawn, and if I were not dying—you might have stayed here on my sofa, drinking beer and burping to mark your territory.

I'm a sloth, it's what we had in common. And the fact that our left eyes feel much more connected to the intuitive parts of our brains than our right eyes do!

Also, the first time we made love, I remember how we talked about the fact that bulls are really color blind, and how a red garment has nothing to do with their rightful anger. How just having to cope with a cape being waved at you by some short murderer dressed up like a kid on Halloween would be bad enough.

The young doctor took my pulse this morning, prescribed yoga. He had stubble on his shin, and Teva sandals—like you. This guy, this doctor, made me blush when he said he liked my cockroach tattoo. He walked out to get the nurse, held her hand and brought her in to see it. She had a cute hair cut, neon-blue eye shadow. She laughed, said *random*. I told them why cockroaches fascinate me, that they can live for weeks with their heads cut off.

They looked at each other, seemed to connect without touching—as if this were all about them.

Day of the Renaissance Fair

It's the day of the fair, and my friend Vicky's cousin Kyle is sneaking looks at me, flushing and grinning when I catch him, his teeth spaced far apart and skinny. He wears a shield of armor made of recycled cans. It would have been fine (being gawked at) if it weren't for the odor he carries—a teenage odor I don't feel ready for, maybe a mixture of Extra Cheese Doritos and Brut cologne.

Vicky loves to laugh behind his back, use him for wheels. *Such a freak-face*, she said once, when we saw him walking downtown alone as usual, unaware that his iPod had slipped, his ear-buds dangling down like tendrils. Vicky and I are still content sucking on Popsicles instead of what some girls do—which might be making us mean (the repression and stuff).

He's already given us money by paying for parking at the fair, since he drove. It feels like, no matter what he does, he still owes Vicky something. I admire his responsible attitude, his scurrying around to stay out of our way so he won't seem like a parasite. Sometimes I think, "Play dead, why don't you, while your cousin the bitch uses you, practices her diva skills."

"Oh, shit, I didn't bring cash. Kyle, can we have a twenty?" Vicky goes (snorts, wrinkling her pug nose).

"Kyle, dude, we'll buy you the perfect present!" she whimpers, knowing how perky her tits look blooming out of her Renaissance bodice, the fair maiden with rusty lip-goop.

Kyle seems suddenly frantic, his left eye twitching, looking this way and that as though a predator were stalking him. His face becomes the color of a fruit medley (shades of purple, whiteheads, pink spots). His sunglasses show a tiny crack near the frame, as if part of him is broken but he doesn't know it.

"Here," he says, handing her a twenty-dollar bill in slow motion, as if any quick movement might ruin something perfect between them. I want to smear him with kisses, yet I follow Vicky into the trashy crowd of fake jugglers, kings, queens, whores, and clowns. I walk to the food palace court and buy a roasted turkey leg so I can take my time.

I watch Vicky flirt with a tattooed freak selling leather-bound water bottles so she'll get one free.

Kyle doesn't buy anything, and we don't even try to find "just the right gift" for him, either. That night, at Vicky's house, I keep waking up, imagining the leather belt I might have bought.

Last Open

We heard the sound of an opera playing, smelled cookies baking before we crossed the threshold this time, before our realtor, Frances, could pick up three new glossy sheets on 2369 Laurel Lane, gasping at the astounding price reduction.

We'd seen this home before, (it was the very first one we'd looked at) when it was overpriced, and I was just starting to show, had finally stopped vomiting and wishing to die. The seller's realtor, colorful hair extensions, a retro Ozzie and Harriet-style apron, wearing just her socks out of courtesy, appeared from the kitchen. "Welcome, welcome!" she said, shaking my hand limply, then Alan's hand (he wiped it on his pants afterward). "You are ready to pop now, lady!" she said looking at my girth.

Hors d'oeuvres were waiting in the dining room, an open bottle of Chablis. Pasta salad, fresh cherry tomatoes with real basil leaves, anise cookies. Frances, our realtor, said, "Renata, thin as ever. I'm only mad with envy."

"Looks yummy, really," Alan said, with a slight fake British accent.

"Oh look, little tea cookies!" I added, in an exaggerated British, far more cartoonish than Alan's. Alan would have to try and top this next time, if he wanted to play my game. We recently started using different accents in different Sunday open homes now, because it was too funny. Frances paled, looking at me strangely, as if she were pregnant herself, her lopsided furrow deepening. All of the sudden, I wondered if she were married.

"Explore," Frances said. "You two, just the two of you." She winked at the other realtor—they put arms around each other, like best friends, wandered into the warm kitchen. Frances seemed close with all the female realtors we met, though with the men, she was pricky, all business, acted as though she'd never met them before.

Alan started searching for hidden speakers immediately, as soon as we were out of sight. "So goddamn sophisticated out here with their opera in the shitty suburbs, right?"

"And so homey for the pregnant bitch," I added. It bothered me too, the staging, predictable all leather furniture, large vases of colorful flowers in the main rooms. We weren't supposed to use a bathroom without permission, but I was dying.

"Come in," I whispered, pulling him in to the master bathroom, closing the door behind us. "Wow," he said. "Look at this sunken tub shit, like a jacuzzi." We locked eyes while I peed a stream that felt strong as a garden hose, or a horse. I remembered the smell of my mother's pregnant piss. I used to run in after she'd use the bathroom to sniff my invisible brother's or sister's spirit. Mom's pee smell was bitter and peppery, different than mine.

My tits were so swollen they looked like tubers. Even when Alan caressed them gently, they hurt. "Udders" I called them. I loved to say it now. He knelt and hugged me hard while the stream kept flowing, so sweet, I nibbled his earlobe medium hard. "Will you be my mother?" he asked. He asked that a lot.

I could hear the two realtors, talking in full voices about the wonderful neighbors on this block, the luckiness of this particular pricing, the seller's desire to find "just the right buyers for emotional reasons," how quaint it all was.

"I'm getting so hungry," Frances said to her friend. "I think I'll indulge in Babette's feast here if you don't mind." The other realtor laughed. "Miss Frances, who do you think this feast is for?"

I pictured Frances eating, rolling her eyes at the other realtor, stuffing her face. I wiped myself slowly, carefully as Alan watched. "Quilted toilet paper," I said. "Boy, that's nice."

"Nowhere better than an open," Alan said, unzipping.

I looked at us in the mirror, and noticed Alan's bald spot from that angle. This bathroom was for people who came in a kit, who did everything right, whose pee was water, harmless. Taking Alan in my mouth felt as old and comforting as our apartment in the city, its drafty doors, tiny kitchen without a dishwasher. Making Alan happy. Home. He kissed me and told me it was over, we were done with this bullshit fluff.

Screenplays

Whenever I went into the basement my eyes found Daddy's boxes full of unpublished stories, stacked neatly in prim rows, as if they were waiting for him to return from a trip. His clothes were in clear plastic bins. I recognized one of his shirts. It was a long-sleeved T-shirt with a dog on it. I could just see the shape of it at the bottom of the bin. Mom couldn't deal with giving them away. I smiled at boxes and bins, saying in my head:

> *See you later, alligator . . . see you later,*
> *. . . see you later, alligator.*

Every morning, Mom's pewter hair made her look ancient. My stepdad's lousy "I'm a man's man" cologne smell stunk up the bathroom. He worked in insurance and thought he was friends with everyone.

Being a passenger all the way to school in her car was the price of being owned. She would pretend she hadn't been crying. Prattling about this and that. She was clueless about the high-definition TV between us—showing a cheesy black-and-white movie (the kind you only watch in the afternoon when you're sick).

Mom reminded me of those sad-looking leading ladies you catch in noir flicks. Her husband dies, and she remarries a hat-wearing hard-ass geek played by Fred MacMurray (the kind that gets irritated by everything, especially her kid). She predictably turns into a miserable, bitter character. So does her kid.

~ ~ ~

I had an office where I wrote my screenplays. Putting it together every day required patience, but it was worth the effort. I loved the building and the un-building (taking it down before she knocked on my door to say good night). Knowing that it would be stacked under my bed for the next day. It was always there, waiting, unbreakable. I had cut the cardboard pieces myself and they fit together like a jigsaw puzzle.

Everyday after school I went to work in there. I imported a jar of spaghetti sauce, thick Dutch pretzels, black-cherry cola.

I wasn't really sure how I wanted the mother in my screenplay to look, though certainly not old. I wrote the first scene taking place in a beauty salon, the woman's hair being colored a deep mahogany red, her scalp massaged by a stylist. In my mind, I conjured the stylist's face, his attention to detail. The way he'd look at the woman, as if she were important to him. I'm not sure why he'd feel this way about her, but he does.

This stylist becomes her boyfriend. He loves kids, and he trains animals. He lives on a ranch. He smells like pine. He cooks omelets and crepes on Sunday mornings. He talks a little and listens a lot. He puts his arm around you only when you invite him to.

After writing this scene, I felt a longing for the stylist. I wanted him to wash my hair and trim it just so. I wanted to know what he really thought about my mother—the way she looked and who she had become. I brushed my hair out smooth, and the motion calmed me.

The fighting that happened every night like clockwork was going on behind Mom's closed door. My stepdad was saying, "You see? You see?"

Mom crying.

I went to say good night to Dad's boxes. They were dusty. I said good night to them three times—turned circles three times one way—then three times the other. When I closed the door behind me I heard a very quiet settling, like a sigh. I wasn't sure, but I thought he approved of things.

I put the office away and turned on my sound-soother to help me fall asleep. I picked the rain forest setting. Birds were chirping, insects humming. They sounded so real.

The DSL Guy

He came to my apartment to check the DSL connection. Something was wrong—it took an hour to Google a simple recipe for chicken soup. I had a sore throat, was sneezing a lot, and felt tired.

I have a bad cold, I said. My apartment was cluttered—a holding tank for things that had no use. Christmas cards up from three years ago.

Frost barked once. It was an embarrassing "woof" that sounded like the word woof. Then he rolled over and showed the DSL man his stomach and privates. The DSL guy put his hand down for Frost to sniff, and said, Are you the man of the house?

Of course he had to enter my apartment (it was his job). He shuffled his feet and rattled the countless wires in his carrying box.

Everyone's sick, he said.

I was getting ready to move in a few weeks so I didn't really care about the DSL situation long term. Being an only child had at one time seemed a burden—but now that my parents were gone the world was my oyster. At least that's what my therapist said. That's how to look at it. She used those words.

I need it to work now because I'm making arrangements to move, I told him.

It was also because my fiancé Russell liked to e-mail regularly to tell me all the tiny details about his new illness, but I didn't say that. He'd diagnosed himself on the Web, and found out exactly what he had. It's called Reynaud's Syndrome. Sometimes his fingers turned blue.

The tea kettle howled in the kitchen. It sounded like a fire alarm. I ran to stop it.

Where's your system? he asked.

For a second, I didn't know what he meant.

He inched into my much-too-warm apartment. I pointed.

I watched the sturdy legs of the DSL man walk over to my workstation in the kitchen nook. He investigated the wires behind the desk carefully, his ears cocked while he fidgeted.

This will be easy, he said. He looked like he was approaching middle age.

I went to the bathroom and blew my nose. I brushed my hair and put on mascara. I forced myself to look at my throat in the mirror and check for redness because Russell wanted me to list all my symptoms and e-mail them. He was a psychiatrist, and sometimes I wondered. He seemed so nervous about illness—and I hoped that didn't affect his patients negatively.

I listened to the doggy sound of my congested breathing, holding back sneezes for a minute so I could hear the DSL guy.

Done! he said.

I burst out of the bathroom, hoping to get his business card before he got away.

He was already in the foyer, his cell phone ringing. Yeah? he said.

He looked at me and put up one finger in a just-one-second gesture.

I sat on the floor next to Frost and watched him carefully.

He didn't seem to notice that my eyes were on him, moving from his lumpy Adam's apple to his waist. Broad, but not overweight.

No, that's not OK, he said. He hung up and rolled his eyes.

He was not OK about something.

How about a cup of ginger tea? I asked.

Another time, he said, his eyes widening. He handed me his card, patted Frost. We smiled at each other as he left. I breathed out, my congestion loosening.

I went over to the computer and checked e-mail. New from Russell: Subject: Reynaud's Syndrome symptoms.

Subject: Prognosis and care

Subject: Where are you?

The Serious Writer and Her Pussy

The serious writer has embraced the word "pussy." Other words for this part of the female anatomy are repugnant, carnivorous.

A pussy has a life of its own. A secret life. One can smuggle drugs inside a pussy.

As a serious writer, in mid-life, she must master speaking the word "pussy" with confidence and authority. She practices doing so out loud for her next bookstore reading. The serious writer is starting a book tour to promote her new novel which is bursting with "pussy."

She practices reading in front of the mirror, engaging her slightly furrowed brow... medium voice...

"'I love your pussy,' Ian says softly to Trina, his hooded eyes at half mast," the serious writer reads to her refection in the mirror.

"'I love cock,' Trina offers, imagining his range of movement."

Her dialogue is raw. Edgy. The serious writer is known for this.

"'You're huge, Ian... my my my...' and she is touching it through his cords. She is feeling its neck, perhaps its beak... but doesn't want to frighten Ian by admitting to her deepening fear...her hunger," the serious writer reads.

"'My god. You're damp,' Ian says, stroking her muff, her moistened ball of hair, the underwear covering Trina's pussy," the serious writer says, her voice tiring.

(The serious writer is sick of the adjective "wet." She is experimenting with other adjectives. She wonders if a man would really say 'damp'... Not just any man... but Ian, the vegetarian with an occasional weakness for farm-raised fowl.)

She looks at her face in the mirror. It is a successful face, one that has accepted three Gertrude Smallwood Awards. A face that should not have any trouble with the word "pussy" for fuck's sake.

"Pussy," she says it again. She says it, right to her face.

Scotts

The first ad I posted on Craig's list Saturday morning was meant for Scott F., whom I work with. The heading, "Do you feel the same way, Scott F.?" I said in the ad that I was having yummy thoughts about him—did he know? Could he tell? I wasn't sure he'd ever look at personals, but just had to try.

An hour later, when I got back in from a run and checked my mail, I was surprised at how quickly Scott had responded.

He said he liked the heading of my ad, and knew right away it was me. He said he liked me too, but he worried if going out wouldn't endanger our already competitive working relationship. So! That was why he didn't flirt with me, looked at me as if I were particle board. It always made me feel unattractive. I had to go reapply my makeup a few times a day. I looked for his non-interest, then took a break and lined my lips and colored my lids brighter.

I responded with a new heading, "I hope you're the right Scott F."

The part I didn't understand, I wrote, was why he felt we're competitive? I mean, we are both HTML coders in a huge company—we work for different divisions. I asked if he had blond hair and a goatee since it would be unsafe to give names or say where I work.

This morning, Sunday, 20 new e-mails from Scotts. All of them with blond hair and goatees, crushed out on some woman at work that sounded much sexier than me. One of the Scotts said, "I imagine your enormous boobs in my mouth and can't manage my staff anymore."

Another Scott said, "I never understood that scent you wear, like a blend of Je Reviens and Patchouli oil."

A sexy looking Scott (a picture of him in bed half naked) said, "I never thought a talented writer like you would ever even look at me, so I'm hard all the time now and in a lot of pain."

At work, I can't look at Scott. He seems nervous, but maybe he always did. He chews his nails and whistles when he walks to the coffee area. It probably has nothing to do with what I'm wearing—or my luminous smile. Now I avoid him, eat outside alone facing the mountain.

I feel like I don't know who he really is. I keep thinking about the half-naked Scott, wondering if I should take a writing class and change my life.

Viking

I tell him he can watch, but he joins in. I wake up imagining him lying next to his wife. He comes here for something wild, our little game. I make him grunt. Later, we'll grill chops.

On Thanksgiving he calls me at midnight to say I remind him of an Al Green song, though he can't remember the tune—it's driving him crazy. He's lost his appetite, his scalp itches, he can't sleep.

What's happening? he whispers.

It's chasing him, he says.

I tell him everything will be OK because I remember a few Al Green tunes. I start one, and he joins.

Little boxes of metal next to our ears are singing, glowing.

Orgasms

Dr. Klein enjoyed an enormous sandwich during the beginning of the session—chewing slowly, then licking his lips for what seemed a very long time. This was the day Vivienne decided to talk about her concerns relating to adopting a dog, though her husband was allergic to animals, and hated disruption (he became irritable when she brought home a cactus with hair).

It was happening more and more frequently. His sandwiches always had raw onion. She couldn't change her 1:00 appointment time. It was all he "had."

"So," Klein said, "I've been meaning to ask you—do you have orgasms?"

She felt her face redden (she was actually planning to talk about buying a dog).

"Do you cum?" he asked, chewing. Masticating. In her mind, she spelled come both ways, thinking while spelling.

She hated the grunting, chomping sounds he made during silences. She missed being young, sprinklers in the summer, Slip 'N' Slides. The sink that always leaked in the bathroom.

"Trying to remember?"

"Right," she said.

"Good. You cum often, I hope?"

Many people wanted to work with Dr. Klein since he had achieved minor celebrity with his popular self-help book, *Becoming Your Own Muse*, and appeared on the *Today Show*.

He was the therapist who suggested she get a dog. But now he wouldn't talk about dogs at all. Every session, he brought up some part of her sex life—how she felt about her husband's sexual performance, what her history was before her husband...

Vivienne noticed that Dr. Klein's eyes would linger on her shirt when she was free-associating. This—mingling with the smell of onions, and his breath from four feet away, was making her shy, repressed, ill.

"I don't come very often," she spurted, spitting a drop, saying it.

He smiled kindly, almost priestly.

"What I really wanted to talk about is how much I want a goddamn dog," she said, breathing through her mouth, shutting off her nose completely. "And that I'm pregnant." Her voice came from a lower place in her chest she'd never heard before, almost guttural.

He looked at her, wiping his chin with the back of his hand. He took his pad and pencil out from the hidden folding drawer inside the arm of his leather chair. The pencil was attached to the pad with a string—a set that came together, maybe a special order for therapists.

The onion smell was back even though the sandwich was gone—now just a tiny invisible glop in the doctor's colon. Vivienne looked at the rug for stray ringlets that may have fallen near her feet. Nausea came so quickly.

She pictured the dog as she heaved, protective and warm—could hear his throaty bark.

Bird Refuge

I spend weekday afternoons at the bird refuge, watching the ducks and geese. Today, I talk to a guy named Mike, who I saw here yesterday. He tells me about himself, how he used to work for the zoo, managed the zoo-mobile rides. I loved those as a kid, I tell him. Then we start talking pleasantly about zoo animals and idiotic parents and their smart-ass kids, and we talk on this subject for a surprisingly long time. He is funny and cute—but I'm getting cold, and it's late. The sun is drooping way down toward the ocean.

I slip off my shoes and massage my toes, while he watches me rub them. They hurt when I'm angry and upset; my acupuncturist says I hold stress in my toes. "Don't go barefoot here, you can get an infection from bird shit that will eat your flesh," this Mike person says.

He sounds like a guy who is good at knowing about rare diseases, that kind of thing, something in his voice like a growl. I feel tipsy from the schnapps, and because I've been jilted by Jake and I want him surgically removed like a wart.

Mike wears hiking boots, has full, puffy lips, and just one arm. His left sleeve hangs off. I don't look at it directly, just out of the corner of my eye. I try not to notice. He's probably sick of people noticing and pretending not to notice. He probably hates me for my lack of forthrightness.

I put my shoes back on, tie them, say, "That's what I need, my flesh eaten," and he smirks.

The duck nearest to us has only a few tail feathers, looks obscene and naked, compared with the rest, and basically stays clear of other ducks. It squawks to tell the others to fuck off. I try to imagine what ungodly trouble could have left a young man like this Mike with one arm and hiking boots.

"Do you drink too much?" Mike asks.

I tell him that I am not drinking, and that I don't. He shakes his head and smiles with cute little gappy teeth. I pull a beer out of my lunch pack and imagine fondling Mike's groin. He skin looks baby animalish, and I want to say something intelligent.

Suddenly, I wonder what he is doing here alone, feeding the ducks. Probably, like a freakish person—he is just acting queer as hell because he's already been labeled by people. Nothing matters, is my guess.

"What happened to the arm?" I ask.

"You are pretty," he says.

He clears his throat, and says he'll tell me about it if I meet him here tomorrow not drunk. A feeling of anger overtakes me, starting with a tingle in my fingers, working its way to my cheeks. Perhaps this man is a creep, just a pervert feeling sorry for himself.

"No promises," I say, walking away, skating through piles of new bird waste.

Kona

I take the napkin and wipe my lips, glance at Mom pouring Kona–her holiday splurge. Straight from Hawaii, she brags, winking. As if it were illegal.

My step-father puts his weight on our least stable chair, leaning it back. He wants to break his ass so we'll have to feel sorry for him, wait on him. The dots on his shirt are retro sixties style, and he looks like a cartoon salesman. The type in the New Yorker cartoons, the loser who uses his family to build him up, even though they're so tired of him they could puke.

The cigarettes I like are the kind that kill you the quickest. Filterless and manly. I pop my knuckles watching him sip the Kona. He takes it in as though weaning, his puffy lips sucking against the rim of the mug. The Wall Street Journal next to him for comfort.

"Goddamn paper's soggy again." I bat my steam-green eyes at him so he doesn't tell Mom to fuck the paper boy again.

He puts his foot on mine and smiles. "Leave this old man alone," he says. I know he wishes he were a cool dude I could think something of. I'm wearing my mistletoe earrings to work. He thinks since I've moved back home, he has a right to me. Likes to call me "hobo."

Mom is extra peppy, she's been spiking his coffee with her anti-depressants for four whole weeks, in time for Christmas. She says she barely needs them—he does though. He made fun of her for taking them. She told me one night when I was puking in a bowl having gotten too drunk after work. She pulled back my hair like when I was little. When the vomiting stopped, said she's started spiking Tom's coffee.

"Are you going to kill him?" I asked. The room was yellow.

"Not yet," she said in a flat voice. We didn't snicker, or maybe we did.

Birds

The fourth month, one of her tricks was being his nurse. She would bring a towel and put it on his forehead. She noticed he preferred pencils to pens, made shopping lists. "Please, please buy these things!" the lists would say at the very top. She could see he erased at least half of the items. Q-tips for paint brushes, the list would say.

Later, he'd paint with them, make homemade paint from coffee grounds. He painted birds, mainly.

"Honey," she'd say, "this is better than anything."

"Please," she almost said, "teach me."

They were in line for a movie when she felt her dress was beginning to pillow. It looked like a dishrag covering a small bowl, but she didn't say anything about it, and all that mattered were his brown birds. The way he believed in vitamin D and ultraviolet rays.

The Landlord

I smooth my hair, lean my cheek against the wall to chill. He wrote a note next to the emergency numbers, used the clown magnet, stuck it on the fridge. It said, for crying out loud, he's letting me live here cheap, letting me use his car, his CD player, his lotions. It's time. Says he's falling for me, even though I'm a walking disaster. Those words.

I walk out of the bedroom I rent from him. I pay on time. He's lying on the sofa, bare feet hinged over the arm. A dish of cocaine and guest spoons dainty on the coffee table near the fruit bowl. I bend down to tie my shoes, say, "Hey, turn on the Jacuzzi, I'll just run out for cigarettes."

He slices a sleepy-bear smile my way, my mouth stretches sideways and upward like a circus trick.

You Should Know This

The first time our parents left me in charge, I was twelve, nearly thirteen, old enough to make sure nothing went wrong. They dressed up in clothes I'd never seen, went to the opera in a flurry, as if escaping from hell.

My little brother, Finn, and I watched two hours of Comedy Central, ate chicken nuggets and thawed peas.

Around eight o'clock, his bedtime, I told him he was adopted. He was six now and should know this, I said.

He grinned, doing the crazy tap dancing routine Mom taught him. Shuffling off to Buffalo.

"Mom said you had to be nice to me," he said.

"Well. Finny, that's what I'm doing."

He loved dancing, as though he had batteries—could do it all day, all night. His feet were on all the time.

"You lie," he said. "You just don't want to be my sister." Finn could be a very unattractive child.

"Don't you think I was there when it happened? Don't you think I helped them pick you?" The phone rang. Neither of us moved to get it. Finn's feet stopped and he stood rock still.

"Why did they pick me?" he asked, his nose starting to drip. He needed a haircut, though he'd just had one. They were trying something girlish with his bangs.

"Because you are both wicked and good," I said.

I went to the kitchen and poured him a glass of milk.

"Your arrival was a blessing to them, Finn," I shouted from the kitchen. It seemed too quiet, though it always did without Mom and Dad fighting. When I was Finn's age I'd seen them hugging from their door crack. He was squeezing her like a boa-constrictor, she was gasping for air, trying to stay alive. They were naked, and I didn't know if I should do something to help—so I stayed and watched the rest.

Back in the living room, it was dark. Neither of us thought of turning on the lights. Finny was walking around the living room like a little bird, following the circular pattern on the braid rug. Perhaps he was thinking back to his birth trauma. His real parents. He sat on the rug, limp as a piece of overcooked pasta. Thinking about what to do next. I studied his shape, the bull's-eye part of the braid hugging him in the dim light.

The Mask of Politeness

There are whispers about the new young architect; they say he's brilliant! They found him in Boston. There is a congratulatory Dim Sum lunch the day he arrives.

My fingers flail around the keyboard, botching letters, legal documents. He likes me, hovers near my desk, says he hates his new Los Angeles view. Doing anything Saturday? he asks.

I'm open, I say.

He arrives at my apartment, roses and apologies, acting late even though he's early. I show him the dump I live in, babble about my crazy roommate who takes photos of me asleep.

I show him my tiny room.

After dinner he takes me to his parents' home in Torrance where he lives for the summer. He admits that he's sitting on his father's credit card; it's giving him a sore right haunch.

Nothing about the house he grew up in stands out—it's one in a row of plain beige houses with manicured front bushes. When we walk in, his grandmother smiles, is giving herself insulin. She is older than anyone in the world, bent over, tiny as a bonsai. The rest of them turn toward me as if I am a piece of sharp bone that made its way into the dinner soup. He sticks me in his bedroom, tucks me under his coat, and runs out to explain.

The divorce is in the works, but it takes a long time. I can hear them whispering angrily. I feel like a prostitute, eating Saltines on his rose colored sheets. I open the prim dresser, touch his perfectly folded shirts. Everything about him is threaded, counted, purposefully sewn.

~~~

Once we've escaped to a hotel by the beach with the shades drawn, the mask of politeness is gone. Underneath is a starved beast. His skillful fingers erase all the partitions between our clothes.

Laughing, I run and hide in the empty coat closet. He has to collect me, make love to me amidst the screaming coat hangers.

Villa Monterey Apartment, Burbank

In California the earth shakes, Ma said yesterday crossing an
invisible line from Nevada into California. She pushed the
gas pedal hard and the car almost jumped. I clapped for her.

Today Ma's meeting with a real estate company to ask for
a job so I get to stay at Tanya's apartment and swim. Tanya is
the beauty in the family—fourteen years older than me. She
has a bronzed face, streaked hair—is addicted to the sound
track from West Side Story. Her boyfriend, an actor named
Sam, smiles at me. He has dark muscles, swimming shorts,
Popeye shoulders stretching out against her avocado shag
rug. He just got a part in a TV show.

Can you walk on my back with your little bare feet, honey?
Sam asks.

My dad was old and always looked hurt—I'd hurt him by
being so little and clumsy. Once he taught me a lesson about
it, and I never touched him again. Maybe Sam doesn't know
how bad I am.

Tanya won't talk about Dad, she hates him so much—so
I pretend I never knew him when I'm with her.

She's not to get hurt, Sam! Tanya barks—a hundred years
crawling into her voice.

Oh, come on! She's a kid! he says, blowing air.

I don't want to hurt you, I say. He stays quiet, waiting. Stepping on him feels soft and hard, squishy. You win, Tanya says. You both fucking win.

Tanya is so much older than when she left home to become famous a year ago. She walks out swishing a bright red towel behind her. She's going swimming.

A kid can't hurt me, he says.

~~~

In the pool, they don't talk with words, just touch each other's faces bobbing up and down in the deep end. I pretend it's a movie. Seven short palm trees stand in a line behind the pool deck as if waiting for autographs.

Mom once told me smog is invisible once you're in it. She's right. Everything sparkles in Burbank: the Vacancy sign on the apartment building, Sam's neon goggles, the two lines of pool water sliding from my sister's bloodshot eye.

Slices

"Porcupines float in water," Dad says.

He always says shit like this. I have my period and hate the thought of quills and liquid. Everything smells wrong.

Last night, Brett was hating me again. Why he hates me at night, I don't know. So, it makes me sick. Those bloated nights, the way gravel can move into my mouth.

When Brett does me it is eight minutes or so of feeling connected to something that fits.

"I am your flutter face," I say, to stop Brett from saying anything about my ugly face... or else, to make him say it.

Dad says my shoes suck. "They are kid's shoes. How do you expect to get anyone to love you back?"

"Okay, then give me some money and I will own four shoes, instead of two," I say.

He glares at my shoes. "You would not know what the hell to buy. Why would I do this for you?"

One time, Dad stood there studying us girls, walking out of school together in a herd.

He said, "Everyone but you looks like a stick figure inside of a fuck 'n flip book."

That was the day he said I was "meaty-fine," which meant

the fattest, which was true. I felt sorry for my friends—appraised like that. They may really be made of paper.

Dad is fat from lack of air swishing past, he moves so slow. He has toothpaste forming like a greenish magic rock on his sweatshirt. Calls it "Mount Rushmore."

"Someday a plane will land there," he said once after his third.

"Yeah, with twenty snow troopers."

I'm exotic, Brett tells me. "The kind of girl-thing that can eat rubber off a rubber plant," he says. I guess he means I make do with what I have and not complaining a lot. I hate that he thinks that, as Dad does, as they all seem to.

Brett says I am the kind that could survive in a desert in the summer, barefoot.

"You are the type who would die on the first day," I said.

"Good for me, then, goodgoodgood."

I felt like washing him away—on hot and then on spin, until the fibers of his brain were so dry they cracked.

He has seen me bend and sway and not spit. He got used to that. It was my own fault. Too many people fly around my head, taking tiny slices. They don't admit it—maybe they don't know what they are doing. I only know because they are swollen when they are done.

Salty

It was when she loved a man with eyes like a fish everything changed. With his kisses she would swallow clear water. Fear would rest behind colored pebbles, be gone for entire seconds—long enough to bubble inside and out. I love this, she spit, swallowing his air, his name, dancing backwards with it in her lips.

Plump and Interesting

She hoped he would smoke a pipe, smell of tobacco. "I'm plump and interesting," she told him. They'd never met, and she loved to lie. May have been the wrong thing to say. Not many like plump... She craved the swell of relief on a man's face.

It's No Wonder

Unfortunately, slept with Eli again, but at least I know why: if I think back over the week, I had toast on Monday, pizza on Tuesday, a huge subway sandwich on Thursday, bread roll and a Danish on Friday for lunch, and then pizza again last night! It's no wonder.

Sunday, I wanted the slap of Eli's thighs to calm my carb attack. He wanted the same.

Nancy (his wife) was at her weekly Texas Hold'em group, the skinny bitch drinking de-caf and laughing. Eli stuck home with beer and the grandkid's Nintendo Wii for company, hoping I'd call so he wouldn't gorge on sourdough pretzels.

After only one ring he picked up, drove here quick as text.

Naturally, I am hoping that using the elliptical machine at the gym twice a week and being somewhat "coy" next time with Eli will mean that I won't store as much water as usual near the holidays (bread products and sex make me retain water like a sponge). And with that perhaps I will have lost the desire to ruin anyone else's life.

So the plan is to lay off sex a little, eat a lot less bread and pizza! Avoid the bowling alley, boycott the pasta aisle at Safeway, and stop snacking altogether! I think I will post a sin diary this week so I can pay attention to what I'm doing, try and have vegetable soups for lunch, volunteer at St. Steven's home for the aged, download songs of real French nuns, singing.

Roast Goose

Christmas being the supersized holiday of happiness, my heart felt both slippery and angry as it has in the past. My serotonin began dipping dangerously.

I slipped Eli a text saying, "Big boy, how's your belly?"

Eli texted back, his green bubble said, "Feast me."

His wife had gone to an eggnog and Wii party in Rome. I had been taking seaweed baths, trying not to think about Snickerdoodles, Angel Butter cookies, and Bouche de Noel. Perhaps extra fat strengthens the body against past or future times of hunger.

"So... what are you wearing?" I asked him on the phone.

"Heavy cream," he said.

"And what are you thinking about?"

"Butter, meat, and nuts," he said. "You?"

"Candied fruits, home made preserves, and roast goose," I said.

"What do you want me to do to you when I get there?" he said. He was ready to make for one bloated holiday. I felt myself perking.

"It's Christmas. I want you to cook. I want you to take me apart and put me back together."

Water Damage

He said I should just open the front door and walk in, no big deal, just walk past them in the living room watching TV and act normal. He said since it was raining hard they'd all just be there like slugs on the sofa. Go all the way around, he said on the phone, "Down the hall in the back of the house. My room is at the end."

Just say "hey" like you know them already, he said, they've lost all their brain cells and can't remember their own names.

He was right, it was easy, nobody even turned around or looked at me, and I told myself if that was so damn easy, other things would be easy too. He was back there all alone in a small bedroom with a fan on. The rain was louder in his room than seemed normal, and the walls were bare. His hair was long and girlish and shiny. The bag he took out of his pocket was what I had come for. It would take the worry away, so I smiled at him, for this, and because I always wanted such hair.

He laughed as though he were squeezing air out of his lungs, as if he knew what I was thinking, and said, "You should model, you could be a petite-small type, the type you see in ads."

I said, "Those girls are tall in real life, short girls don't model."

But I could see that I should have thanked him for the compliment, because he started tearing up. His window was open with no screen across, and it was freezing. I realized that he was wearing a T-shirt. There were clothes all over the floor and papers in stacks that looked wet.

He said I reminded him of all the dead movie stars he'd ever thought were beautiful. He was really crying about something else too, he said.

He asked me if I felt my beauty. He was acting as though crying was normal, just another man with long hair crying in a freezing room with a fan.

"Yes," I said. "I know that I am going to die very young because of my looks."

"Right," he said.

"Trouble sticks to me."

He came over to me and hugged me. I wanted that heat a little bit anyway. There is no right way, I told myself, and no right person. I touched the girly hair.

"Like this?" he asked, and I could smell baby shampoo on his neck.

"Yes," I said. I realized he was worried, and he wanted to fuck me while I was still on Earth, but maybe I would have to pay him for the stuff regardless.

"You're a sensitive person," I said, moving in slow motion.

He handed me the bag. I stood there with my hands groping around in my pockets feeling for money.

"Shit," I said, "I've been losing everything."

He brought out his guitar from the piled up closet and sat on the floor. Strummed some chords, la la la all fake like he was Green Day. Threw that hair around like a whip. I almost laughed, but kept things low and slid off my skirt. I played Chelsea Road in my brain as I let him fuck me, looked up at the high ceiling—the oblong spread of water damage.

The Call

There's a hum of electricity before the ring—mimics birds, cheap clocks, Buddhist meetings. It's summer. I'm sleepwalking, holding his phone number like a straight or flush.

The thought like a slap, he's really leaving this time, tells me and his secretary, Jen, in a whisper with scallion and coffee breath near the empty creamer. Jen's lazy eye wanders toward me and away.

I cradle the phone, finger his odd numbers, the seven, the five—as if my forefinger could do this and I would not have to watch.

Emerald

He asked her to choose a shade of green. He liked the way she stooped to tie her shoes like an old man, as though she could fall over very easily.

"Go," he said.

The window was open and she screamed it. There was always a system to his punishments. He asked again.

Card House

Christmas morning I slept late, didn't feel it was Christmas. I had made myself a list of the things that I didn't believe in. My step-brother lived in a cheap brown hat. That was the first thing on my list. He was in Alaska, beating off, he said, and playing the synthesizer while unemployed. He said it last night. That was my second thing.

"Do you have to say that on Christmas eve?" I hissed into the phone.

"Sure, because we love doodads, and I am still a doodad," he said.

I did not laugh.

Once, when I was afraid to walk past a dog when I was eleven, too old to feel afraid, he said, "You are covered in super-tight Saran Wrap."

I walked past that dog so tight and held in place. That was my step-brother, the one that made me brave. He would never wear a brown hat.

~~~

"She tried to kill me once."

That's what Dad said to his girlfriend, the first time we met. It wasn't true. Dad laughed and said, "My little Hun."

I was ten, and Mom had already been gone for a year. I

was running and holding a fork and Dad was stepping out quickly with so much coffee in his type-A blood. Spouting off about Pottawatomie culture, and how we live in a time machine, or something. He hated the president. I hated that he was my father, but would not have killed him. I wanted to make sure he was firm, perhaps. He was the only freak in town who dressed up as a Chippewa to watch the Macy's Thanksgiving Day parade.

~~~

It was hell trying to get my step-brother to crack a smile.

He was unpopular again, he said.

He said, "I am a darting asshole, exactly."

"Who said that?" I asked.

"Nobody."

Pulling at his split ends.

I wanted to say she was a stupid bitch and a slut. This girl from drama class he crawled behind.

His hair was shiny and gold, I envied it, and wanted to touch it—but not him. That night, we watched Masterpiece Theater stoned, Dad was meeting his girlfriend for a retreat.

There we were, acting like old people together again, eating brownies. Then later, I pet him instead of the cat.

~~~

"I want to look like a British World War Two soldier," I told the stylist.

"Oh, excellent," he said, and he gave me a boy's cut. A young and nervous and pimply little boy cut. I looked down to check that I still had breasts.

"I bet you are doing this for a chick," the cutter said, assuming I was a baby dyke.

"Yes, I am," I said.

His cell phone rang. I looked at myself in his mirror and thought, I could do it, I could join something.

~~~

When adults asked me what I wanted to be when I grew up,

I'd say a scientist so they'd leave the subject alone. My future was full of pads and probes and allergy shots.

My stepbrother said he wanted to be a scientist too, when Mom was alive.

After she died, he said "Shut up" to anyone who asked. Even church people. He never answered questions, and people assumed he was slightly autistic.

I would eventually become interested in myself. I told one friend how I would study pollen. I told another friend I would dance. I told my step-brother that we would save the planet by building card houses.

The Chubb Illusion

Sometimes her boyfriend Jon and she would sit on the porch and make bubble cheeks at each other like fatties. Carla would get into a giggle so deep that she would nearly choke.

"What if you die swallowing your own laughing spit?" he said, once. "What then?"

They talked about having a picnic, what they would bring. He said, "Grapes and cheese," and she said, "Boone's Farm Strawberry Hill."

Carla imagined they would squabble over many things if they spent more time together, but in truth, they were seeing each other every day and things felt like they were loosening up, peeling off like skin. Underneath, she wasn't babyish anymore, and neither was he.

They both loved Carla's coffee-table-sized optical illusion book, and would smuggle it outside at night with a flashlight to emphasize the effects. The illusions had names like the Cornsweet Illusion, and the Hollow-Face Illusion, and the Chubb illusion. They laughed at the names of illusions, imagining the people who invented them.

"Lab rats," he said.

He asked if she knew how to bake morning pastries, when they were lying in the yard of freshly mowed grass on a warm mid-summer night, looking at spots jumping off the pages of the book. She told him that she could bake anything, as long as she had a cookbook and the proper ingredients.

"I have an addiction to muffins," Jon said.

"That's okay," Carla said. Right after she said it she wondered if she really was nice, or if that was just the way it seemed to her.

"Sometimes I forget to put on my parking brake," Jon said, touching her hair. Carla's shirt was filmy because it was summer. She wore a rugged sports bra underneath to minimize the nipple effect. Jon's hand slipped under Carla's shirt, under the tight spandex sports bra, found Carla's rigid nipple. Neither spoke for a while.

"I could shriek and ruin this," she said.

"Yes, you really could," he said.

Like clockwork, they started laughing. She swallowed too much spit, then coughed. He laughed so hard too. She wasn't the prettiest girl in the world, but he loved the part that only came out with him.

Leaving Hope Ranch

My friend's father moved away one year, leaving her in a huge house in Hope Ranch with her mother and two teenage sisters who tortured her.

"How do they torture you?" I asked, hoping she would tell me this time.

"Lots of different ways," she said. She stuttered slightly. Her nose was long and unusual. Everything else about her looked perfect.

"They take my fingers and bend them back. Last year they broke my wrist," she said, poking through my backpack to find my lucky rabbit's foot. At twelve, my friend already had a curvy body, but insisted my shapeless one was perfect. She tried to hide her nose with her long dark hair.

"Where is your dad now?" I asked. Both our mothers kept shaving mugs in the back of closets. We had this in common.

"Tyler, Texas," she drawled, in a phony, coquettish voice.

When I slept over we watched TV, running into the kitchen for brownies during commercials. Whatever was on Fright Night would get us squealing under one blanket, hiding our necks from vampires. I hated it when her pretty sisters wandered in while we were watching TV just to call her "Pee-

Butt" and "Doo-Doo." That was as bad as they got when I was visiting. They smiled at me hard as they left the room, throwing their hair in loops around their long, gorgeous necks.

One morning, as we were washing our faces, my friend told me I was going to be pretty. I didn't say anything, for I was curious about it myself. That spring my face had grown bigger and sort of interesting from the side.

"What do you want for your birthday?" she asked.

"A rock polisher, but I think they're too expensive."

She looked away quickly, then turned back with cheeks that were warm and wet.

"My mom has cancer," she said.

She explained that her father was coming and that they would fly to Texas together. That way she could get used to living there in the summer before school started. We wouldn't be able to see each other, but she would write to me.

The day before she left for Texas we didn't know what to do—so we lay in my yard on beach towels, tanning. Rubbing Coppertone on her back, I admired her smooth skin. I spread the lotion in deeply because this was the last time. I made myself look at her. From here, she had already become a woman.

Separation

My husband is reading on the bed. After packing my third bag, I find myself staring at his penis which pokes out the side of his shorts when he lies down. It has always been friendly. I'm going to miss it.

"You are staring," he says.

"Yep."

"Still leaving tonight?" he asks.

My stomach is rotted out from too much coffee. He gets out of bed, grabs at a Kleenex box behind the bookcase. His clam-shell mouth closed and round.

The telephone rings.

Four miscarriages in the last two years. Each time we adopted an adult cat. Four cats now. One of them, the gray tiger cat, is dozing on the foot of the bed.

"I am but. . ."

"Remove Zelda," he says.

I pick her up and take her to the sunny living room. On the bed, when I come back in. . . his shorts are off, not his shirt. His right hand is already moving evenly, tenderly. He seems to want me to watch, is gazing at me with a tiny smile, so I unbutton my shirt for him. His sperm is rising—hopeful and stupid.

The room smells like fresh bread.

Terribly Light and Small

Joshua and I are standing in the apple area, sniffing before picking which ones to buy. This is our Saturday night routine, gets us out of the house and social. What was once a regular type of grocery store, is now a national chain.

A young woman with corkscrew curls offers samples of acai berry spread, grins at us with closes lips. Her T-shirt says "acai pie." Joshua stares at her, the aisles going by too slow. I'm walking as quickly as possible without hitting shopping carts.

"I'm cold," he tells the bright containers.

"Yay," he says.

Nine years ago, I skied in the Sierra Nevadas—four months pregnant. They couldn't stop me. I loved to be cold then too.

Three massage chairs near the bathrooms where quarter elephant and car rides used to be. Lavender soap and towelettes for customers. Down the "Healthy and New!" aisle, Joshua points to organic mango/mint/cocoa bean energy bars, crispy chips made from soy beans and green tea powder. "Pretty," he says.

Because he's terribly light and small, I pick him up and put him in the cart. He cackles maniacally. I do not look around. The word "antioxidant" is displayed everywhere you look in here, like mouse ears at the Disneyland Hotel.

He points to the vegetable area, ruby grapefruit piled up to a peak. Joshua gets caught in patterns sometimes and his eyes play dead.

Later, I'll open a bag of cardamom mint chips and eat them one at a time sitting in the rocking chair, waiting for his breathing to even. Flecks of flavor come out like stars—a minute or two between.

Zelda

My sex drive walked back in the door with a broken suitcase. Her name was Zelda. She was sort of the new me. I called her Zelda, as though I were a maniac with two selves. During the pain syndrome, the real me had slipped away. My husband had stopped noticing that the me was gone. I bored myself to tears. The real me was unrecognizably plump and asexual.

Not Zelda. She wanted my physical therapist's body, the one named Brian.

Sirens were often bursting past our window, ruining people's lives. In the paper, a letter about how people were getting hit by cars just crossing the street to collect their dog's poop. That was exactly what had happened to the real me. I had been hit by a car. I didn't remember it, but that was what happened. I cut out the article about drunk tourists and put it on the fridge.

"It is more dangerous to cross your own street than to fly over the Rocky Mountains in a two-seater," the article said. The real me understood and empathized.

Zelda said, "So what?"

That's what the physical therapist said too, on my first visit to him months after the accident where the drunk tourist nearly took off my leg.

"So what?" he said. "Here you are now. You are you in this moment of being you." He offered me some peanut brittle. Said it was the only thing he cooked since his wife left—and he loved the melding of sweet and salty.

I told him my marriage was storming. I should not have said it, but I did. I cried on the massage table. He rubbed herbal oil on my neck, gave me his "overview" about husbands. I was enjoying his fingers, and the sensation of warmth.

"Husbands suck when wives are seriously hurt," Brian said. Zelda was somewhere nearby, listening. Brian took a picture of my damaged leg, said he liked the shape of it—named it "Matilda."

"How's cute Maddy today?" he would say. I refused to look him in the eye, because doing so would make me blush. I still couldn't exactly walk.

My friend Sandy brought over corn everything and flirted with my husband wearing bright purple lipstick. Corn dogs, corn cakes, corn bread, corn chips, corn litter for the cats. She believed that corn meant good luck.

Sandy had both kinds of arthritis. The long term kind, and the surgical kind. She popped Advil and always carried something made with organic corn in her big purse. Her boyfriend hated children, would not walk within a block from a school or playground. She'd finally left him, but now her knuckles were purple and she couldn't work. My husband called her a "champ." My husband said her attitude "rocked."

There was a heat wave the day Zelda burst in, didn't knock. Sandy had stopped bringing corn products and was now bringing soy—leaving strange soy snacks in the kitchen along with the web of her perfume.

My husband was taking care of himself in the shower. I heard the shower running when Zelda sat on my bed naked and frowning. Her plump, shapely 1930's legs were steaming. White, white skin. She whispered and winked at me, nudged me to call Brian on his cell phone. A number he had given me one time, the time he told me he wished he could kiss Maddy.

Brian answered with a yelp. It was probably his dog. Did he have a dog? He probably had a house. I imagined him in a bright yellow kitchen with nothing to eat. He said I should come in for a followup, and that he had a quiet evening ahead, he could open the place up. He could make time.

He said, "Ultrasound is delicious." He said he'd bring peanut brittle, as though that would be the best part.

Sex In Siberia

My imaginary man lives in Siberia. We touch down on each other like helicopters. I smile, move my mouth around him— offer a warming hut, a place to explode. When he bursts, storm clouds open.

Southern California boasts mild, featureless people. The Weather Channel's talking heads, all botoxed and baby-fatted in their cheeks, ramble on about radical snowstorms in New York State. I paint leaves, collect Styrofoam in buckets. Driving downtown for wrapping paper, I count the fake blonds wearing two dollar Santa Claus hats.

My parents divorced and nobody yells anymore, but that is no longer important. I want a Siberian life, a Siberian husband. One whose hair changes from brown to light.

My dog seems worried, and so, he and I take long walks. Sweat trickles down my back. The dog pants miserably. I promise him that someday, we'll skate alongside a large man who loves Labs.

In December, I slump into bed early, imagine what it will be like—Siberian sex. Better than any other kind—so cold outside, so warm under the covers. I ball up socks and rub them where the man would go. We're there, and he is teaching me how to taste snow.

Camp K.

Soon, she will allow the other campers to know she's not fucking around, this is life! She is still young and attractive, and can play bingo with a large group of night people. She looks better than most women her age with a beer, arm raised.

One silly loose ceramic tile in her front yard left her widow to a sweet, pot-bellied man (her husband, Jim), who died on the ground from a brain bubble, while an army of white coats moved around him—picking him up like a toy and taking him to a vehicle. She remembers the medics as a swarm of ants eating elderberry pie.

At breakfast, she is almost alive, and still, she feels like eating the other campers. She hates them and their laughing. She does not know why her friends said she should be ready for this, for a vacation by herself in a place of sectarian forced fun, such as Camp Kierkegaard, or whatever the fuck they call it. The camp and its cool-assed multi-stalled bathrooms, and bare "cabin" look and feel. Expensive, and still, they appear to be sharecropper shacks. They could be filmed in black and white with some rickety looking, skinny child-model standing on the slat porch holding a broom.

Instead, it is inhabited by traumatized urban couples, here to escape life grinding down around them. They hang out by the lake talking about France—slathering SPF-50, comparing water sandals, hanging up their dry and wear while cocking their heads sensitively.

After breakfast she will listen to her CD with sounds of rain, insects, and goats bleating. An Irish healer created a series of numbered CDs to make the feelings of a widow less dangerous. She holds the promise of this around her middle like a warm cat. Somehow there's the sound of crickets now when saying hello to people over pungent eggs and potatoes. She can sit alone or in a community with others and listen to her own, special moods—smoothing a worry stone and a bottle of ketchup.

Blood Sugar

I miss the Bob who would admit he loves fudge sundaes.
Yesterday, Mom said, "Where's your bliss?"

"Hiding under my lumps of cellulite," I said.

"Excuses," she lobbed back. She's had her eyes lifted so
high since her surgery, she looks feline. Life feels like being
stuck in a bus, next to a skinny bitch—the kind that keeps
blinking.

These are the "love replacements" I imagine swirling
inside my mouth: Pizza with everything, meatball sandwiches
from Ernesto's, triple-cream brie from Safeway.

"It's about shooting high," Mom said. She's planning her
next vacation involving dolphins, her current obsession. She
wants, well, it's her "life wish"—to ride one, and last time
she sprained her ankle just walking to the dolphin-riding ticket
area, tripping on a toddler.

Usually, I walk in the park right before dinner, to improve
my outlook. I try and ignore the puppies getting training
treats, their owners cooing, Goooouuuud Girrrrl. Yesterday
I snapped—bought a corndog. I licked it to make it last—so
slow the sun went down and I didn't notice it had become
night.

I don't think Bob's home, he never is now, but I could

call from a blocked number and check. He's lost so much weight; he's sprinting to the front of the meetings for achievement buttons, thanking God and whole grains for saving his life. The women always giggle, though he says the same shit every time.

"I have choice," Bob's new T-shirt says.

All I have to do is choose water over cookies, celery sticks over pancakes. Cortisol has elevated my blood sugar levels, which may be why I dream about men, fat ones and thin ones, with delicious smells, yeasty as fresh dough.

The Ernesto's delivery man comes wearing a Hawaiian shirt and flip-flops cause it's still summer. He says, "We count on you as much as you count on us," instead of, "So, what's up with you?"

I've started tipping a dollar less, and next time he comes, I'm going to let him take it from my hand.

Shoes

It was hard to find the right shoes. Jane needed to talk to a human on the telephone at an online shoe company. She would ask intelligent questions about stability and comfort—and even if the person were dumb, she would still be accomplishing something, finding out what mattered for fragile feet.

The online shoe store had a phone concierge service called "Core Value Talks With David." It was free. Well-made boots had core values, she had core values, and David (whoever he was), obviously had core values or they would not have hired him to take these kinds of calls.

She dialed the 1-800 number on the screen.

There was no ringing, just music, the Dresden Dolls—then a recorded voice that said, "You have exactly five seconds left on hold," (which seemed unnecessary) and then a live male voice.

"I've never been into shoes but I am now. Good evening, my name is David. How can I be of service tonight?" the voice said.

"Did you say that you have never been into shoes but you are now?" Jane asked. Her hearing wasn't perfect since her last sinus infection.

"That's my script," David said. "And who with the lovely feet am I speaking with tonight?" he said. "First name only, please."

"Well, sure, hi and good evening. I'm... " She looked at her feet, her lovely little feet that had been through so much hell, and a few depressing sexual encounters since her divorce. New middle-aged men had sex issues that came with instructions, pills that could be fatal were often needed by these men. Just to make love to a woman!

"I'm... Miranda," she lied. "Mandy," she said, "Or you can call me, Minnie."

"As in.... mouse?" the voice said, sounding a bit happy with itself, maybe arrogant.

"Of course," she said. "Now, David? If that is your name, I wonder about your core values immediately, if you are reading to me from a script, and if you are assuming that I like to be connected with Disneyland. My life is not at all connected with Disneyland, David, and I am not with polka dots."

She took a swig from her light beer, and felt a hovering sensation in her scalp.

"Well, my my," said the voice. "Who's having some issues?" He sounded like a mediocre psychotherapist, and she wished, that magically, he could be. "I'm just having an 'in the moment' reaction to your fake approach to customer service, David," Jane said.

Jane felt hungry suddenly for a briny pickle, so hungry she couldn't focus on why she had called. She no longer cared about stable shoes. She was low blood sugar.

Neither of them spoke for at least twenty seconds. She could hear him breathing evenly.

Jane said, "Kid, listen—I'll call you back."

"Otay," he said. "Call me anytime, we're here twenty-four hours. I'm Core Values at extension #403."

~~~

The next time, when she reached the voice named David, she got right to the point. "Why do you work for a shoe company if you are not into shoes?" she said.

"I've never been into shoes, and I'm still not," David

said. "And my verbal introduction is pretty much real—it's better to let the customer know that we're not shoe whores here. We're educators."

"Sure," she said. "David, here is my take away. I am just one of a hundred voices on hold, and I really think that since I told you my name was Miranda, and that my nickname is Minnie, we became way too casual, too quickly."

"I think what you need to understand, Minnie, is that I understand that core values are deeper than the shoes we wear, and that's what I'm here to say, Minnie. Minnie, I can help you select the shoes that will make you feel grounded, and also, Minnie, I will make sure you get free shipping and overnight delivery free—because you deserve it Minnie...

"Don't we all? Don't we all deserve wonderful service... Minnie?"

Jane was surprised that David, who had last time seemed people-sensitive, had disappeared, and was now behaving more like your basic dime-a-dozen shoe salesman.

A passionless David.

"Yes, we do deserve to be treated well, David. I believe we do, David," Jane said, suddenly angry, and wishing to kick him.

Her name was not Minnie, and his name was clearly not David. David was such a lovely name, she thought. The perfect core values name. A founding father's name, or a dead lover's name. She thought about how she might have named a child David.

"Are you suggesting that free shipping will give me emotional comfort, David?"

Jane felt out of control of her kick-ass voice and her moving lips. Jane could imagine David desperate for a cigarette.

"I need this kind of understanding, this sense of value, of real core values. And I'm grateful," Jane added in a lower voice, a feeling of alcohol's warmth bringing in some friendliness. Also, just a bit of curiosity. A child's kind of innocent curiosity.

This David was cute, real cute, she could tell.

"David?"

"Yes, Minnie?"

"David, I was wondering if I could ask you what your real name is?"

"Oh, (he jumped right in) David. Really, they were only hiring Davids."

"So, if your name had been Gaga, forget it?"

David laughed. A real laugh. "I wish my name were Gaga," he said. "Nope, it's David, and I think if I called myself Gaga it would sound pretentious."

Jane laughed too, though that wasn't anything she had been suggesting.

"Here's a little bit of information, David Gaga. I've got a filthy mind, and I imagine you are very attractive."

"Hmm. What size shoe was that, Minnie?"

"I've always been a night owl, David Gaga," she said.

"Minnie, these phone calls may be monitored for quality assurance," David said, in a low voice, not a whisper exactly, more like a moan.

"Oh, you are under watch," Jane said, imagining an enormous room full of cute Davids, some Davids watching other Davids. Some Davids less intelligent than others.

"You are welcome to detail your foot width and shoe size in an e-mail to me directly at stevego@gorkish.com Did you get that, uhm....Minnie?"

"Sure, Steve, I got that, and will do so now," Jane said. She pushed End and the phone was silent. Jane looked in the bathroom mirror, and gently touched the smile lines like commas around her lips. They were nice lines. She would love to know more.

In This Light

John does not own a wall mirror. "Sorry," he says, "we can use each other's eyes to know we are human, okay?" He does not believe in reflections.

There are drops of semen on my lips when he says he loves me for the first time, and tears. I do not dry them.

~~~

Twelve hours after my husband David and his bike were destroyed by a truck, people distributed hospital smiles. My cheeks smiled back, bile gathering inside my throat.

Congratulations, you are now a bird with no tree.

They'd thought he was dead, then changed their opinions and had something to say to me when they found me sitting against a wall in the waiting area hallway. He was alive. But not his spine.

"You may have heard it wrong the first time," the hopeless/happy face of the doctor/nurse said. Someone held my hand, my hands.

~~~

David had been home with twenty-four-hour care for just over one year when I started walking alone in the city in the middle of the night. For some reason I felt an urge to buy milk in the middle of the night, which we were never really out of. I was not frightened under any circumstance.

One of the many nights, walking alone in midtown at 2 a.m., I was held up at gunpoint. A group of youths with hanging jeans swimming around their knees blocked me, squealing, "Who the fuck said that?" They took my money, and one of them poked my nipple. I felt as though I were watching it happen a short, safe block away.

John owned the Ice Mart where I bought the milk. Every night he was there, listening to music on his iPod, talking to the few slumping, tired customers. He always stopped talking when I came in, said, "Hello, nightingale." The night I was held up, John looked at me very hard... but didn't ask what had happened. He offered me Kahlua, and I cried a little. We sipped from the same small bottle—watched each other's lips.

Maybe my cell phone knew something beforehand, because it vibrated often and for no apparent reason.

Now, John vibrates, I vibrate. I crave his lips, his eyebrows, the smell right below his stomach. What it makes my body feel, so stupid, so young.

~~~

David molds delicate cats and birds with colored clay. He can use his fingers very well now.

"His fingers do the walking!" the day nurse says. This nurse, Jill, a handsome and strong girl, has full breasts. David's eyes rest on the window.

Behind his wheelchair, on the wall, a photo of us newly married. Goofy, grinning. Redwood trees. I am wearing the felt hat with the little pink cloth rose. David always said it made me look like Clara Bow.

"Okay, well, I'm off to finish up some stuff at the office and grab some supplies," I say. "David, you take care of this fine girl." Jill is used to this line, nods.

"Sure thing, and David will be very happy to see you tonight," she always says.

I kiss him on the head before I leave. He says, "Aaaah, aaaaah."

His lower body is covered with a thin blanket, and this way, I do not have to see.

Jesus Suckmint

If they were to make a TV movie of my life, they would make the first scene with me in a plane—smashed into the window by a business fatty, raising and lowering both legs over and over. He would have the same fucking thing my screeching grandmother had—the thing she lubricated her life with.

I remembered how Grammy folded one leg over the other and said, "Jesus-suckmint." She was put on earth to suffer and I was put on earth to watch. She was always sucking cough drops when she said two swear words together. The combinations were endless.

During summer vacation, while my friends were in Hawaii or Italy, I flew to New Jersey and looked forward to my cousin's hollow chest cavity. We giggled about Grammy, touching each others knees carelessly and rolling our eyes at each other. The way was to make the best of things... to not complain... or ask for a different seat.

Delivery

Tony delivered all the pizza orders to our neighborhood near the ocean. No other place delivered this far from downtown, and Tony did that for us, six nights a week, in his Tercel. His brother Richard had recently died in a car wreck, and before that, Tony and Richard tag-teamed. Tony's father owned the restaurant.

He'd hand me five extra takeout menus, and say, "For your lucky lovers."

The women at the dog park would hassle each other about him. The dog park chicks called him Hotslice.

One evening, after a delivery, he asked me if he could smoke on my front steps, and I said, "You never need to ask, just light up and have one, and can I join you?" I was eating delivered pizza every night, just to see him.

After he left, I brought out a roll of paper towels and cleaned my front steps of pollen, dust and disgusting little insects. I wondered where my pride had been all these years, why I hadn't wanted my front door to seem friendly and charming....

Another night, I invited him in to share the Vegetarian without onions, and he said he had nothing else to do, no more deliveries to make. We sat in the living room and didn't say a lot. What felt important was enjoying the pizza, his pizza, my pizza. Pizza that had been delivered to me by him and now eaten with him.

"I love the thicker crust," I said, taking a slice. He nodded his head. "It's so, so gooey," I added, and he smiled at my face.

He told me I was pretty, and asked me if I liked green olives or black olives better.

I said, "I hate green, but love black," which was absolutely true. He kissed me, and I tasted black olives in his mouth. I imagined black olive wreaths on his brother's casket. I wanted to taste them strongly, and I knew what sad men needed.

He left the next morning. During the night, when he was asleep, and I should have been, I walked around and looked at his things. Leather jacket. His cell phone. It felt warm.

Vegan

Beth had glitter makeup that someone gave her. I wondered who. It was still sealed, she'd never opened it, and it was in a small box of unused makeup—stacked with other belongings. I knew she would want me to have it now, so I brushed it over my cheeks and eyelids. It made me look alive, and I smiled at my face in the mirror. It was still my face—a face that was born looking spoiled.

"Don't ever talk to me about boys or meat," Beth said on her last birthday.

"You mean men?" I asked.

Beth forgot we were grown up a lot. Nothing mattered as much as the fact that she couldn't find any size twos and I was trying to help on the Internet. When we were little, her hair smelled like teriyaki chicken. I remember telling her as though it were the highest compliment. She pulled my arm so hard I never wanted chicken again.

"How would you like to be fried?" she had said. She was a vegetarian, a vegan, and eventually bones and skin.

The doctor said it was not because of her diet, it was her brain making her body die, and then it finally did its job. One stupid nurse said that to my mother, about her brain being in charge. Mom turned to the chair Dad would have sat in, and said, "See?"

Air Quality

I remember the way she leaned into her knees, breathless, sitting in her mother's semi-private room. Her purse had a crushed flower petal design.

She'd asked to consult with me directly before the admissions release—told the nurses I seemed the expert on bi-pulmonary embolism, her mother's condition. Surprised, I explained how I was just one of her mother's five docs—taking information to prescribe blood thinners.

"Well, the point is that I love nice doctors," she said, her teeth white as gurney covers. Clearly, they were bleached, though I'd come to expect that. Tea-stained smiles were a thing of the past.

Days jostle along, one day and then the next one shoving after. I think about what I might have done or said, even how I'd sound saying it, the exact words I'd choose.

I would have asked her to step outside for a breath with me, regardless of air quality. I would have let her know how a blue pen exploded in my pocket moments after she left.

Surrounded by Water

"We live in a state surrounded by water," I'm saying to nobody in particular, mixing an Amaretto sour.

"And most people never go to the beach," he finishes, as if he were my oldest friend.

Working in this bar for a while, making pretty good money, I'm still thinking one day I'll see him and know his face when he sits down.

"Did you want extra sour?" I ask.

"Perfect," he says, flipping his thick black bangs. "And when you catch a little break, you want to join me?" he asks.

"I don't sit with customers," I say. I always say.

Lou Anderson, deep into the regular, shouts, "She's too fucking important; she's a dancer."

"Nope," I say to Black Hair Amaretto. "I'm just a nurse."

He smiles with tight closed lips, salutes. We look at each other for a sec.

His phone rings, the James Bond jingle. I giggle, then stop—his face whitening like a bleach stain.

"Hello... Hello, hello, hello?

"Wrong guy," he says into the deep, deep phone. "Fuck-off, jerk-wipe.

"Pardon my French," he tells an invisible person sitting

next to him, throws his fancy phone into the trash can, our trash can—rimming it, near the register.

"So, you're a real live dancer?" he asks me as though I'm a black phone too, smashing his fist on the hard wood counter.

I look through my eyelids to check who's around. If maybe Tim, the bouncer, sees. Tim's moving toward us in slow-mo, there's enough in my peripheral to breathe now, though I pee a little in my pants anyway. The other guys, my regulars, sit very still, sucking their skinny straws like air.

Reservations

Toni remembered how, on their first date, she and Tom traded tongues at a French Restaurant, told each other, "No, no, no..."

Tom had laughed at her bout of hiccups. She squawked, holding her breath.

"Done?" Tom said, smiling.

A nice looking silver-haired couple walked past their table, following the hostess. Their teenage daughter tagged behind them, pretty and angry looking—her cheeks red.

Tom's gaze followed the girl.

Tom said he was a magician, demonstrated how to fold a cloth napkin into a hat.

"Ah," Toni said. "Perhaps, but..." She sketched a big-lipped woman on the cloth hat with her dark blue eye pencil.

His eyes flickered even when the low-breasted hostess walked by. She had a parrot voice when people came in, said "Good evening, do you have reservations?"

"That's funny," he said. "We got in without reservations."

He leaned forward. Toni kissed his mouth. His breath reminded her of frosting from the bottom of a glass bowl.

Irina's Hair Shop

Irina cut our hair when we lived on the hill. She was a blonde Russian woman who wore pale powder, fake eyelashes, and blue liner. She rented the tiny beauty shop on Polk—two chairs near the window, turned away from the sun.

One cut she told me about her ex—how he left her with no money. Their teenage son was taller than her now, and stayed with his girlfriend too often.

Men all want one thing, she said. Even my own damn kid.

That time she styled my hair round like a mushroom.

My husband Leif and I were still newlyweds who stacked tofu boxes and refrigerated safflower oil. We lived next to a Chinese beef jerky factory. Toxins floated in our window. All the newspaper stories were about cancer. Skin cancer, throat cancer, pancreatic cancer. We didn't have enough money for furniture, much less cancer.

Leif became irritable the day of his trim. He swore while he was shaving in the morning, cutting himself more than usual.

What's the matter? I asked.

She flirts with me, he said.

What a bitch, I said.

I imagined him a small child on the beach at Long Island Sound, his mother leaving him alone for a sec while she put on her suit. Something about Leif was unnaturally vulnerable. He had serious asthma most of his life, and lived with too much worry.

We went together. When she saw me, her face reddened. I picked up a *Vogue* and sat quietly while she cut his hair.

You two are like a comedy team, she said.

As if to illustrate her point, Leif told her a joke about how much hair he was losing because of my tofu lasagna, my tempe casserole, the lack of meat in our diet as if I were poisoning him. I felt my hands get cold—though I tried to fake a chuckle.

Irina laughed so hard she snorted, doubling over as though she were losing urine. She cut his hair deeply, winking at me grotesquely. When we walked out Leif was nearly bald on one side.

A week later, walking to the health food store, we noticed her windows were taped. A sign in the door said "For Rent." The shop was dark.

We saw it as somehow our fault, purchased expensive algae tablets from the health food store to fight off cancer. We swallowed bits of ocean each morning before opening the windows.

Thirty-Nine

He's tan. I look down at his large bare feet and he invites me in for burritos. The sun is setting behind the university where I picture him too often. The light is jabbing my eyes through the window, and I'm squinting—accentuating my crow's feet.

He throws a towel on the curtain rod to block it.

Better? he asks.

Last time I came he told me a story about a rat his friend bought in Hawaii, mistaking it for an exotic dog. We were laughing, laughing, and this is how we explained how it started.

I haven't told him I've started real estate classes. After twenty-five years devoted to acting classes, auditioning and insomnia—I'm ready to stop. He thinks I'm a great actress, comes to see me in local plays. He brings flowers every time— stands backstage blushing as if he's the luckiest person to know me. He's in his third year of medical school. I've just turned thirty-nine.

He unbuttons his shirt. His chest is lithe and healthy. He's got real definition, and it's almost too strange on him. He must be working out—something he said he didn't believe in, just like he vows to never live a conventional life. He thinks he will escape it all and be an honest country doctor,

159

living in the mountains somewhere with animals and kids. His is still a child's face—interested in everything.

You're looking, he says.

I'm going to, I whisper, and once again we are doing everything we shouldn't.

~~~

While he showers, I notice my eight-by-ten glossy taped to the wall near his closet—the headshot taken of me three years ago with stage makeup and lighting. I look like a movie star. The photographer was so expensive I had to sell my grandmother's table to have them done.

When he comes out of the bathroom a halo of steam follows him. He looks at me as what's next? Is there more? The way a kid begs an Oreo after dinner.

You still like that photo? I ask. It looks nothing like me.

When you're famous, how will I prove I knew you if I don't have your photo?

What if I don't become famous? I ask.

He dresses more casually than ever, Hawaiian shirts and flip-flops. He's not into pessimism. Everything lies ahead of him.

That isn't possible, he says.

I've taken my bag and earrings and am walking out.

Hey, he comes after me and stops at the front door.

What did I say?

Backing the car out of his alley, my music on, I lean into the wheel's movement. I drive. Near the university, patches of students stall near the coffee-shops, gaggles of girls yucking it up—boys gesturing wildly.

Turning right at the river I stop and walk along the bike path to catch my breath. The wind, as usual, gusts strongly when walking directly north. I have to push against it to move forward.

What He Was Like

When he was younger, he wanted to be a dentist. His squint was because he was going to be rich. He had a millionaire's mind, he said, cutting my toenails with the cuticle scissors, collecting my nails in a cup.

He promised me that when I grew up my grin would be even. Nobody would call me vampire. I didn't think he was smart enough to know, but I hid that from him.

My wrists were tiny as a doll's, he said, and sometimes I'd hear him slam his door just to get my mother to come downstairs, to get out of bed and use her feet. In a falsetto he'd sing, "There's no business like show business," and I wondered if he were gay.

I noticed boys and their thick legs that summer, how they'd gather like elk. Sometimes their smell was audible, you could hear in their voices what they tasted like. I tried not to furrow. They loved convertible cars, things that changed. My brother had a rude gesture that he only used when one of them would call and ask for me.

"The climate is changing," he said one night, crying, so I squirted him with my water gun.

To Do List

1. Wake adolescent with softest mom voice, tell her it's time to get up and ready for school. She hates to be late, even ten seconds, because she hates to be noticed.
2. Cereal and orange juice are ready, you say.
3. Cut puzzle pieces of parboiled meat for sick cat, microwave low, re-animate, sprinkle cat vitamins, serve on cat tree.
4. Measure out dog food, mix with pumpkin and green beans for dog diet.
5. Use kitty voice. Isolate other cat in bathroom with stars of kibble.
6. Prepare for drive to school by finding keys and sunglasses in purse despite the stain remover stick, planet stickers, half-eaten food bar, lavender hand sanitizer. Hiding like thieves, keys often play this game forever.
7. Talk to dog about losing things all the time. He is the most well-adjusted creature in the house. Offer volume discount for this service itemized as "dog love" (note to self— always talk to dog).
8. Calm the surly adolescent who used to be your adoring child.
9. Put on function face, lip color, deflate hair with water— forgive it.

Foreign Accent Syndrome

At the dog park, I saw her walking her mother's Yorkie. I hadn't seen her in over a year. I had always admired her eyebrows, simple even roads on her face. Her lips turned down, even when we were kids, waiting for lemons.

She told me about her foreign accent, and not sleeping for three years. These things add up, leave their mark, she said, in an accent that sounded like fake British.

Everyone knew the head injury from the car accident nearly killed her. She'd been thrown—they found her nearby. There was a name for what she had. She said the neurologist explained it so well, Foreign Accent Syndrome. Most people thought she was a bitch as soon as she said hello.

Would you like to come over later and hang out? I asked. I had nothing planned.

She seemed pleased, wrote down my phone number and address.

I'm not very modern, I'm afraid, she said.

Her fancy-sounding accent whizzed overhead like a dragonfly—harmless, colorful. When she smiled, her lips changed direction, charged up her cheeks.

Later, she arrived on her brother's old moped wearing wasabi-green clogs and a backpack carrying all she couldn't hold: Slippers, backgammon board, tea bags, a dainty spoon for stir.

I never lose, I told her after the first game. She cried. I made tea with honey, she put on her slippers. I put on mine.

Lost and Found

house-painter card
T. looks like the man called "House Painter" on the Dream
Date Card my friends and I played when we were twelve. We
sit on the cold fire escape. Smoking. Watching the whores
curdle and separate.

rat
I bribe T. to my loft with a bag of sunflower seeds. A futon,
dust mites, overdue plays. Empty shells.

ring tone
One night I make my phone's ring a Medieval Druid Rap.
He is acting like those poor fireflies I caught and jarred as a
child, though he hasn't lost his flashing eyes. Yet. He wants
to die cute. Like River Phoenix. His ice-blue cell phone in
his back pocket like folded money.

list:
almond massage oil
almond sunset tea
dark chocolate 80%
dry rhubarb soda

lavender bath oil
musk candles
red light bulb

found memory

What's his name took my hand, led me to the bathroom, opened the door and slipped in behind me. The bathroom was dark. "Mari," he said. Through the window I saw file cabinets lined up in black, like widows. It was an office building, the late shift.

how we survived

We made calls, sold diet products. All of us were actors or models. Carla was the token "real person." I hoped she'd invite me to a real house for Thanksgiving. She had a real house, a real husband, and two real kids. I gave her Three Musketeers during break. I couldn't figure out why she wanted the late shift.

mari

He unzipped. "Mari," he said. His tongue tasted like fruit and tacos. Sweet and sour and rude.

sometimes

I can remember his name. Sometimes it escapes like a bug. He was so tall and stupid. These qualities often came bundled together. He (what the hell was his name?) wanted me because I was:

a.

b.

c.

d.

locked

Outdated things make me sad, like the word "howdy." Inside

my life are moments nobody wants to remember. My jaw gets stuck in sleep, by the morning nearly locked, dreaming about the twisting coil cigarette lighter my father had in his car.

benadryl

I answer, in case he's decided to come for Thanksgiving. His friend is still asleep. He took too many Benadryls, he says. He knows because he saw the package floating in the kitchen trash.

"Not enough to kill himself," he said. He coughs, says he wants to come see the cats.

dressy beagles

We're sitting on the sofa in the den just a few feet from each other, holding the cats and turning on the laptop.

"Pick," I say.

He types "dressy beagles" into the search bar.

Four guys dressed like soldiers holding Beagles in pre-Civil War southern belle costumes. Bonnets and velvet dresses with leg holes and collar trim. The beagle's faces fall, but the men are smiling.

MEG POKRASS writes flash fiction, prose poetry and makes story animations. She was an editor for *SmokeLong Quarterly* and now serves as Editor-at-Large for *BLIP Magazine* (formerly *Mississippi Review*). She designs and runs the well-loved Fictionaut Five author interview series for *Fictionaut*.

Her work has appeared in over to one hundred online and print publications, including *Mississippi Review, Wigleaf, The Pedestal, BoundOff, Keyhole, Annalemma, Smokelong Quarterly, elimae, Gigantic, Gargoyle, Prime Number, Women Writers, Istanbul Review, 3AM, Foundling Review, Mud Luscious, Juked, FRIGG,* and *Wordriot.*

Meg's work has been nominated for Dzanc's Best of the Web, the Pushcart Prize, Wigleaf's Top 50 Flash Stories, and showcased for Dzanc Books' Short Story Month. Meg teaches writing privately, speaks to graduate writing programs about new writing, and leads flash fiction workshops nationally. She lives in San Francisco with her daughter Molly and husband Doug Bond.

To keep up with Meg, visit www.megpokrass.org.

Aside from his travels, **TOM DOLAN** photographs Boston and Harvard Square in Cambridge. A graduate of Harvard in the 60s, he spent some time as a grad student at the University of California, Berkeley before recognizing that he wasn't really meant for academia. Retired now, he spent most of his career writing technical and administrative manuals for a couple of Fortune 100 companies, taking up photography as a hobby along the way. His photographs have appeared in online and print publications in the U.S., the United Kingdom, Brazil, Poland, and the Netherlands.

Of the cover shot for *Damn Sure Right*, he says, "I look for little moments like this that contain disparate but oddly complementary elements, like the mesh stockings and the solid brick, the firmly planted foot and the dangling hand." He especially likes capturing moments of serendipitous wit, as in his shot of a (painted) Charlie Chaplin tipping his hat to a (live) couple passing by.

CPSIA information can be obtained
at www.ICGtesting.com
Printed in the USA
BVHW081734180920
589086BV00002B/174